I0841034

Mist and Mystery

Stories, Articles and Reviews

by

Arthur Machen

Darkly Bright Press

Mist and Mystery
by
Arthur Machen

Catalog Number 015

ISBN: 979-8-9863904-1-3

Publisher's Cataloging-in-Publication data

Names: Machen, Arthur, 1863-1947, author.
Title: Mist and mystery : stories , articles and reviews / by Arthur Machen.
Description: Includes bibliographical references. | Cochiti Lake, NM: Darkly Bright Press, 2022.
Identifiers: ISBN: 979-8-9863904-1-3
Subjects: LCSH Fantasy fiction, English. | Short stories, English. | Paranormal fiction. | Essays.
| BISAC FICTION / Literary | FICTION / Short Stories (single author)
Classification: LCC PR6025.A245 .M57 2023 | DDC 828/.91209--dc23

darkly bright
press · design

www.darklybrightpress.com

Contents

Introduction

"And here, though we are initiated in the mysteries, we are assuredly not in the mists."

I

With this deceptively simple statement, we are ushered onto a new journey into unknown regions where wonders await, yet the path is narrow and fringed by veiled dangers. Fortunately for us, there are few guides as experienced or intriguing as Arthur Llewellyn Jones Machen, a man of Gwent. In this new collection of rare tales and forgotten articles, Machen directs us through mist and mystery to "a secret path leading to an undiscovered country."

The precise distinction between mist, recalling man's loss of paradise, and mystery, the pursuit and recovery of it, is not a trivial matter in Machen's work. In fact, these themes and the contrasting results serve as the great concern throughout his fictional narratives. *The Great God Pan*, a harrowing parable illustrating the dissolution of personhood, finds its overturning in *The Great Return*, a tale of fallen man and creation transfigured. This contrapuntal relationship between noetic horror and holy dread distinguishes Machen in the crowded field of the speculative fiction of his time.

In other words, here there be dragons and dragon-slaying.

Some of the many dragons we will encounter are the sham religious sects swirling about as yellow fog through gaslit streets. While it is true that Machen briefly participated in some occult circles in the early twentieth century, there has remained a tendency to both hyperbolize and romanticize the extent to which this represents Machen's worldview. This caricature disappears as Machen's beliefs, clearly and consistently expressed as a critic and essayist, are examined.

For example, Machen routinely disparaged spiritualists as naïve at best or frauds at worst, while never dismissing the danger of their activities. While subtly questioning R. H. Benson's conclusions as to the agency behind spiritualistic manifestations, he nonetheless agrees with the novelist in principle.

"I should think that the author has mingled a good deal in the circles which hover about the foolish and forbidden and dangerous thing called 'occult science.'"

If the misty forgeries of the occult are swatted away, what can mystery offer in its place?

For Machen, the pursuit of ecstasy, an uplifting of man from the dross of common life, represents the right-ordered desire for transcendence. An incessant drive in man to return to paradise remains, and is, in reality, the impetus for art and literature. This theme of return is constantly repeated in rhyme throughout our stories. Written in symbols, it is found in the quest for the Cup and the quest of Don Quixote. It is found in all human expression: *"And poetry, too, is symbolical: it is a collection of sensuous images which are really 'words' in the secret language of the spirit."*

Whether it be occultism, materialism or Freudianism, man is confronted by distorted imaginings which confuse his vision: *"The discovery that Beauty is to be found in shapeless disorder is wholly modern."* However, Machen stubbornly fails to lose his hope for recovery: *"...the secret has been kept; that in spite of the yearly, monthly, hourly work of the enormous machine that we call civilisation, the human spirit yet remains, unchanged and unchangeable, ready, when the opportunity occurs, to wipe out all the lines that have been ruled for it, and to write again the ancient hieroglyphics in place of the modern commercial hand."*

In spite of the many perils which face us on our journey home, we never cease seeking Avalon, wrapped in glory and mystery beyond the next hill.

II

Between the late 1880s and early 1920s, Arthur Machen periodically joined the ranks of various journals, magazines and newspapers to support himself and his family. After earlier stints at *Walford's Antiquarian Magazine* (1887) and *Literature* (1898-99), Machen would would hit his stride as a contributor, first to *The Academy* (1907-08) and then at *T. P.'s Weekly* (1908-1910). Some of his best essays were written for these two periodicals, but the working climate was not always pleasant. At the former, Machen consistently ran afoul of the editor, T. W. H. Crosland, a man who clearly lacked sympathy for Machen and has been described as "a dogged, but quaintly childish enemy" (Reynolds and Charlton, p. 106). The end came when Machen discovered that his salary had been cut. Accordingly, the frustrated writer quit.

Fortunately, Machen would not be out of work long, and there is evidence that he had more than one option from which to choose. At this time, we find Machen successfully submitting work to major publications including *Vanity Fair;* however, he had steady employment in his position at *T. P.'s Weekly*. Founded in 1902 by politician and journalist Thomas Power O'Connor, this magazine covered similar cultural and literary subjects as one would find in *The Academy*, but from Machen's point of view, it constituted a lower quality than his previous journal.

According to Machen's biographers: "...he never ceased to refer to it in his letters as The Lousy Weekly, but it seems hard to make out why" (p. 107). It is difficult to disagree with their expressed confusion. Machen was given plenty of space to write about his chosen topics, and there is no evidence that he faced malicious editors or was ever threatened with dismissal and reductions in salary. Alas, there is too little information concerning his days at the magazine, so in the best of Machenalian tradition, we are faced with an insoluble mystery.

However, Machen's opinions on his new employer and the work are certainly not lost. On the negative side, we turn to a letter written to his friend A. E. Waite. Dated November 2, 1908, it concerned Machen's willingness to write about Waite's theories centered on the Holy Grail, a subject which interested both men greatly.

"...so that I could present your case in your own words to my intelligent readers of T. P.'s Weekly. And since they are so intelligent: You had better not go beyond words of two syllables!" (Selected Letters, p. 46)

Again, it is not known why Machen bore such prejudiced views against the magazine and its readership. Yet, however accurately or unrighteously held these opinions were, the quality of the work submitted shows that Machen did not shortchange his employer or the consumer. Each installment finds Machen at the top of his powers as a critic in both social and literary spheres, and as a stylist in phrase and structure. Cogent arguments and discursive pathways make for a pleasant journey as the reader follows Machen charting a course as wonderful as any of his excursions through the Welsh countryside or the mystical streets of London. Before he wrote an intoxicating series of memoirs in the 1920s, Machen wrought similar enchantment in the pages of forgotten periodicals including this "Lousy Weekly."

To further stress the quality of his work during this period, we may turn to Arthur Machen's remarks on his tenure at the magazine. At first, it may seem counter-intuitive to regard the opinions of an author concerning his own work as useful for objectivity. They may be overly full of praise in one instance, or despairing in another. Too often, Machen thought too poorly of his abilities, and while the self-deprecation he expressed is entertaining and sympathetic, it often misses the mark as in the following snippet from his introduction to a British reissue of an early romance:

"The Chronicle of Clemendy was printed in 1888. I read the proofs with pride. I don't think I did much more than glance at a page here and there at long intervals during the next thirty-seven years. But I held the belief that it was a good book, up to this year 1925, when I read the proofs for this present volume." (p. vii)

He concludes that some things are better left at the bottom of the sea.

Yet, a year later, he did not write so harshly on the material he penned for *T. P.'s Weekly*. That year, he would write another introduction, this time for *Notes and Queries* which sourced its fifteen entries from the periodical. It is a delightful volume, and its quality helped to inspire this current book. The following quote is illustrative:

"Now it is said that if a man thinks at forty as he does at twenty, he is either a genius or a fool. I do not know whether this dictum apply to forty and sixty; but if it does, I deny it altogether. I know I am not a genius; and I don't think that I am absolutely a fool. I find myself in pretty general agreement with every opinion that I advanced nearly twenty years ago; and avoiding all extremes, conclude that I was then and now a fairly sensible fellow." (pp. ix-x)

He then goes on to mention several of the included essays and continues their arguments. While he does not outwardly commend his writing, it is self-evident that the principles and style of the work go side by side. In other words, in a rare instance, Machen finds no ground for complaints.

After reading *Notes and Queries*, I agree with this assessment. The wonderful volume is uncommon today for it was issued only once in a limited edition of 265 copies. After searching through Machen's sizable body of work for *T. P.'s Weekly* which was not included in that rare collection, I felt the need to present *Mist and Mystery* as a way to gather sone of this fugitive material. Most of this work has not been available to the reading public for over a hundred years. It is an open invitation to recover both mystery and romance.

III

From a thematic standpoint, this new collection of rare Machen material has been built with two purposes in mind. Firstly, as a volume of selected short fiction and essays, *Mist and Mystery* represents a modest attempt to follow in the tradition of *Dog and Duck: A London Calendar Et Cætera* (1924), *Dreads and Drolls* and the aforementioned *Notes and Queries* (both 1926). Each of these classic books is a selection of material originally published in periodicals, with the third collection sharing *T. P.'s Weekly* as its source. Secondly, this new volume continues with the survey of Machen's periodical work which began in *A Reader of Curious Books* (Darkly Bright Press, 2020). In most cases, these short pieces have not been available to the public since their original publication.

The Fiction

To open the collection, Machen treats us to a light satire, **Scrooge and the Spirit—Of Psycho-Analysis**, which first appeared in the December 8, 1923 issue of *T. P.'s and Cassell's Weekly*, a later reformulation of the magazine. Though earlier attempts by Machen in the delicate art of satirizing were not often successful, this brief sketch works well as a clever critique of Freudianism while joyfully celebrating Dickens. Until now, this short work has never been reprinted.

Many-Tower'd Camelot (1909) first appeared in book form in the *Notes and Queries* collection under title of *Guinevere and Lancelot*, and is one of two pieces that is common between the two volumes. Here, it appears as it did in its first publication under its original title. This short story was written during, or shortly after, Machen's concentrated period of research into the Grail legends. Although the Grail figures prominently in Machen's fiction, most notably in *The Great Return* (1915) and *The Secret Glory* (1922), *Many-Tower'd Camelot* may be unique in the Machen canon, for he employed the timeframe and legendary characters from the Arthurian romances rather than placing the Cup in the twentieth century. Additionally, the tale's ending may be surprising to readers.

Of the three stories assembled in this collection, **Out of the Earth** (1915) has remained the most accessible to readers. Published after Machen's departure from the magazine, the story may have been the result of a commission from *T. P.'s Weekly* in the aftermath of the incredible success of *The Bowmen* (1914) for the *Evening News*. The story was later used by Vincent Starrett for his collection, entitled *The Shining Pyramid* (1923), before being added to the 1925 Alfred Knopf collection of the same title, which was assembled by Machen himself.

In this latter instance, the story had been slightly revised. Here, the reader will experience the original version with the reinstated numbered sections which are missing from Starrett's. It remains a classic example of Machen's ability to weave a dark fairy tale set in modern and rationalistic Britain. To accomplish this goal, the tale takes a form of storytelling in which fantasy is interleaved with a documentarian approach, allowing ambiguous and mysterious events to break into the supposed normality of everyday life.

Articles and Reviews

Arthur Machen never lost his ability to stir controversy and debate. In 1887, as a young man, Machen had raised the ires of a certain Poe critic in the pages of *Walford's Antiquarian Magazine*, and the ensuing duel lasted through several issues. (See *A Reader of Curious Books*, pp. 15-19.) The first article in this section demonstrates that he did not mellow with age. After a reading Machen's sound thrashing of an article in *The Occult World*, the editor of that august journal could not resist penning a complaint to *T. P.'s Weekly*. The exchange is priceless. Ralph Shirley would return to smite Machen's life once more during the Angel of Mons controversy. Against Machen's claims, Shirley published a thin pamphlet with a thick title: *The Angel Warrior at Mons: Including Numerous Confirmatory Testimonies, Evidence of the Wounded, and Certain Curious Historical Parallels. An Authentic Record.* This tract can be read in Richard J. Bleiler's *The Strange Case of "The Angel of Mons."*

Another article worthy of mention is **G. K. C. on G. B. S.** In this instance, Machen observes and comments upon a long-running debate between two literary luminaries. Although generally in agreement with Chesterton—"he is on the right side—that is to say, my side"—and opposed to Shaw, Machen is not afraid to critique the former's argumentation where he finds it wanting.

Machen's view on the role of criticism and the duty of the critic is well-honed. He did not argue for argument's sake. As the following quote demonstrates, the often curmudgeonly Machen felt compelled to express his deeply held opinions because foundational concepts demanded a strong defense:

"And, though I do not say that the quality of exciting violent disagreement is the one quality of good criticism, I do say that without this quality no really fine criticism can exist. The critic, if he be more than an entertaining chatterer, goes down to first principles, and first principles, on which so many of us differ, are the only principles which are really are worth debate."

Indeed, the nature of good criticism creates a major theme of this book. Below, Machen proclaims that criticism also requires a high standard of ethics from its practitioner:

"Insolence, malignity, offensive personalities are disgraceful in any age, near or remote, and I do not mean by this sentence to imply that true criticism should consist in the mere ladling out of laudatory 'pap.' It is sometimes the painful duty of a judge to order a man to be hanged by the neck until dead; it is sometimes the painful duty of a critic to tell an author that his English is faulty, his arguments fallacious, and his imagination a minus quantity. But it is never the duty of a judge to mingle with the dreadful utterances of doom sarcastic remarks about the prisoner's inferior social status..."

Other articles representative of Machen's quality as an essayist are the insightful reviews of books by Evelyn Underhill and Robert Hugh Benson, his tongue-in-cheek approach to feminist literature and a rebuttal to a socialist fever-dream. His interesting historical account of **The Holy Sepulchre** is astonishing when considering the short space available to him. **The Genius of Persia** is not only an inspired article, but shows how its subject inspired Machen to write one of his most enigmatic stories. In **A New Year Meditation**, also found in *Notes and Queries*, Machen demonstrates his ability to craft a nuanced and poetic vision of interpreting the world. Also highly recommended is **How To Enjoy Life**, a late piece on the value of humility.

The Literary Week

In addition to regular articles, Machen contributed a column entitled "The Literary Week" thereby granting him two pages of magazine space per week. The column, though staying mostly on the topic of literary happenings, is wildly discursive and shows that Machen enjoyed freedom to pursue his interests. The amount of material is considerable, so I have elected to build a sampling which attempts to show the breadth of the column's contents during Machen's tenure. Though it does abound in delightful obscurities, it should also provide a fair amount of interest to the casual reader.

In one case, I must make a confession. The article masquerading as **"The Blue Saucer of Bristol"** is, in fact, a long excerpt from The Literary Week. Its subject deals with a supposed contender for the Holy Grail, and Machen's comments are reminiscent of that excellent trio of essays, *The Sangraal*. I felt its topic and treatment deserved more attention. May I be forgiven this bibliographic impertinence.

Christopher Tompkins

Mist and Mystery

Stories, Articles and Reviews
by
Arthur Machen

Darkly Bright Press

Mist and Mystery.

Though there is a certain similarity of sound there is no real etymological connection between mist and mystery. A man who sees the external world mistily, or vaguely, does not necessarily see it as a mystery.

And, as a matter of fact, the great mystics, as distinguished from the muddleheads with whom they are sometimes confused, have usually been singularly lucid persons.

There can be no higher mystic doctrine than that of the lines:

> Our birth is but a sleep and a forgetting;
> The soul that rises with us, our life's Star,
> Hath had elsewhere its setting and cometh from afar;
> > Not in entire forgetfulness
> > And not in utter nakedness.
> But trailing clouds of glory do we come
> From God who is our home.[1]

And here, though we are initiated in the mysteries, we are assuredly not in the mists.

Arthur Machen

---

1 From the 5th Stanza of *Ode: Intimations of Immortality from Recollections of Early Childhood* (1807) by William Wordsworth.

Part One

Fiction

Scrooge and the Spirit—
Of Psycho-Analysis
By ARTHUR MACHEN

Scrooge woke up with a sudden start. He heard the bell toll one.

He remembered that it was Christmas Eve, and that he was going to make a tremendous day of it with his nephew and his niece by marriage.

There was a woman for you! As hearty as old Christmas itself, and the very wife for Fred.

He had a trifle or two in the pocketbook in the old desk at the foot of the bed that he thought would please her: a diamond and ruby ring that would look well on her plump finger, and a watch with curious enamels on its case that had taken his fancy a full month ago.

And as for Fred: the portly gentleman who had called on Scrooge just a year before turned out to be an old-fashioned wine merchant in an old-fashioned place right down by the river, where they burnt candles in the counting-house all the year round, including the sunniest days in August; and he had supplied Scrooge with a dozen of most particular port, which had been sent to Fred by the carrier.

And Bob Cratchit and Tiny Tim were to enjoy such a Christmas as they had never dreamed of.

So, on the whole, Scrooge had gone to bed in a happy humour, feeling that he was entitled to a good night's rest.

And yet he woke up with a start and a shudder as the old clock in the old church tower hard by tolled one.

"Dear me!" said Scrooge; "I wonder what woke me. But what a horrible smell! Odd I never noticed it before. There must be a dead rat behind the wainscoting. Really, this is dreadful!"

"It is not a rat," said a voice at his elbow. And a dismal and hideous figure stood by his bed. "I," said the Phantom, for such was the form, "am the Spirit of Christmas as it will appear when psycho-analysed. Follow me."

With a dreadful sinking at his heart, and involuntarily stopping his nose with his fingers, Scrooge accompanied the spectral presence. They were out in the streets.

It was Christmas morning.

The people were hurrying to church with cheerful faces.

The merry bells filled the air with happy sound.

The Phantom drew Scrooge into one of the churches.

It was all gay with ivy and green holly and shining red berries and bright tapers. The organ was playing, and they were singing of Peace on Earth and Goodwill to Men.

"Amen!" said Scrooge under his breath.

"Look," muttered the Spectre, "this is a cultural festival. You see, it is the period of the year when vegetation is at its lowest ebb. The ancestors of these people, seeing that the ground was hard and the leaves fallen and that everything seemed dead, were afraid that nothing would ever grow again."

"Phantom!" gasped Scrooge, with trembling accents. "Spirit! speak the truth, I adjure you! Is it possible that even ancestors were such infernal fools as that?"

"Certainly," replied the Spectre. "You will find it all in the textbooks. Mark the result. The cultural feast called Christmas was instituted. The green boughs and the red berries are a mimetic appeal for the revivification of Nature, similar to the mimetic appeal of the may pole. The organ is an imitation of the warm south-west wind; and the singing mimics the twittering of the birds in spring."

"But what are those candles on the altar for?" said Scrooge in his bewilderment.

"You seem a most obtuse person," answered the Ghost. "Midwinter is the darkest time in the year. Candles are lighted to make the sun shine again."

"There must be a dead rat somewhere," murmured Scrooge under his breath. He was still holding his nose firmly between his two fingers.

The church with its bright tapers and red berries and green leaves faded away.

The Spectre and Scrooge were again in the streets.

A poor woman, wan and thin, shivered in the cold December air, and drew her scanty shawl closely about her. She looked sadly at the happy people hurrying to their Christmas dinners.

Scrooge seemed to hear her murmur to herself about the happy Christmases when she was a child, and her poor father and mother were still alive. Just then a kindly looking old gentleman went up to her, spoke a few words in her ear, and put something bright and chinking into her timid palm.

The tears were rolling down his cheeks as he hurried away to avoid her grateful words of thanks.

"That," said the Spectre, "is an instance of the Terror-Complex. Rich people are in continual dread of a rising of the class-conscious proletariat, and such gifts are an attempt to buy off the infuriated people."

"It is odd," thought Scrooge to himself, "how that dead rat—and he must have been dead a very long time—seems to follow us everywhere."

Again the scene changed. The Spirit and his companion were in a cheerfully lighted drawing-room.

A happy-looking woman drew her two little boys about her knees as she sat by the blazing hearth, and began to tell them of the Shepherds and the Wise Men and the singing Angels.

A rosy-faced man came in at the door, humming an old Christmas carol. "Oh, do hush, papa," said one of the little boys. "Mamma is telling us such a beautiful story."

"Aha!" chuckled the Ghost. "There you have the Œdipus Complex. Note the hatred of the sons for the father; note also —" And he whispered in Scrooge's ear.

"I'll swear there are a dozen dead rats somewhere," thought Scrooge, as his gorge rose.

And then Scrooge woke up, and this time in real earnest. He leapt out of the bed and found a little book on psycho-analysis, that had somehow got into the room, lying on the floor.

"And I thought it was only a poor dead rat," said Scrooge, as he took up the book with the tongs and flung it out of the window into the gutter.

MANY-TOWER'D CAMELOT.
By Arthur Machen.

Upon a morning in May a man kept his master's sheep on the hills that are above the Forest of Dendreath, in the midst of the Isle of Britain. It was very early in the morning when the man came out of the shelter that he had made between two rocks, and the dew was thick upon the short grass, and at the sun rising all the land glittered as if it had been the Shining Isle beyond the waves of ocean, and an odour of sweetness rose up from the region of the leaves. Then the sun ascended in his splendour, and the mists in the forest vanished away, and the shepherd saw before him all the wonders of the Forest of Dendreath. In the west he beheld the Road of the Eagle that issues from the waste land of Cameliard; and suddenly he was amazed, for far away he saw a red flame and a white flame advancing side by side along the alley of the wood.

The Flames in the Wood

Now, these flames were indeed nothing but that famous knight of high worship Sir Lancelot, the principal warrior of the Order of the Round Table, and beside him Guinevere, that was to be Arthur's queen. When the shepherd far on the wild hill had seem them they had but come forth from a shade of beechen leaves, and as they appeared suddenly in the open glade the sunbeams smote upon them, and so bright was Lancelot's armour made that it was as if it spouted white fire, and Guinevere was as the burning of vehement flames. Upon her head she bore a cap of golden cloth, curiously adorned with jewels such as rubies and carbuncles and chrysoprases, and her cote-hardie was of red samite. And about her she held a cloak of flame-coloured satin, and her belt was of gold and crystals. Golden was the glory of her hair. So they rode through the alleys of the forest in the sweetness of the May morning, amidst the glittering of many leaves stirred by the wind of heaven. And at their passing by all the choir of the birds of the wood exulted. Deep from the shade in the heart of the forest Eos the nightingale chanted the melody of lovers with unwearied antiphons; to him gladly replied the blackbird, a master of song; the blackcap was of their chorus; from the throats of smaller birds there rose a sweet sound like that of pipes of faerie. So, journeyed Sir Lancelot and the lady by the ways of the happy forest, one glancing gently on the other as they rode at a merry pace.

How This Journey was Begun

Now, when Sir Lancelot brought Guinevere from her father's castle in Cameliard, they rode for a day and found no adventure. But as night fell, and the sun went down, and it grew dark, they heard a noise as of crackling flames, and the sky grew red; and they saw a high hill before them, and on the height of it a fair castle was built, with lofty walls and many springing towers and pinnacles. But a black smoke swelled up from it, and great flames encompassed it, and as they looked there was a roaring and a riving as of thunder; and then that fair and goodly place fell apart, and was dashed down into the dust, being consumed with fire. "Alas, fair lord," said Guinevere, "what castle was this, and who was the lord of it? What evil chance hath so piteously destroyed it all?" "Lady," replied Sir Lancelot, "that I may scarcely tell. Let be a while, and it may be that we shall fall in with some man who shall advise us." And then they pressed a little forward, and Sir Lancelot found a poor man hidden amongst the thorns and bushes by the way, and he asked the man what enemy had come upon the castle, and for what cause it had thus been burned and ruined. "Sir," said the poor man, "ye are to understand that this castle was the castle of Sir Sagramour of the Fair Mount, that was a knight of great worship, and a noble warrior, and the lord of all these lands. And it fell out by evil chance that he saw Eglaise, the daughter of King Ryon of the Rugged Island, as she went forth from her chamber to hear mass, and the hearts of these two became inflamed with love, and so they fled away together and dwelt happily at that castle for a year and a day. Then cometh King Ryon against Sir Sagramour and taketh his castle, and burneth it as ye have seen, and Sir Sagramour is slain, and his wife with him, and no living man is left therein." Then Sir Lancelot and Guinevere, the queen that was to be, marvelled, and went on their way; and said Guinevere: "I see very well that this love is both piteous and cruel, since by it husband and wife are slain, and a fair hold has its portion with ashes and destruction." "Will ye say so, lady?" answered Lancelot. "Consider well that by this same love is all the round earth ordered, with the shining of the stars at night, and with all the spheres of the heavens, and with the perpetual choirs of paradise. And without this love ye are to understand right as the doctors teach us, that there were no brightness of the sun at all, nor any light of the moon; nor should there be any green thing upon the earth, nor any bird of the wood, nor beast of the rocks, nor fishes in ocean; nay, when love shall pass, then passeth man also. And ye shall not say that this knight and his sweetheart were unhappy nor of an ill end, for to our Lord Love they did great worship and great honour, and were well rewarded of him, so that they dwelt for a year and a day in the estate of gladness, and now, praise God in paradise, in the bliss that is perdurable and everlasting." "Oh, knight," said then Guinevere, "I see well that ye are a great lover and a high master—yea, a very doctor of love; and well I wit that in the King's court at Camelot ye have the love of many ladies, and bear the palm of all amorous knights." "Lady ye judge falsely, since never yet have I loved maid nor wife." "Is this as you say, of very truth?" "It is as I have said, lady, and ye must know that I am none of the knights of the bower, but of the stricken field, where

I do battle for my lord, King Arthur, against his enemies, and against the foes of all the land." "Nevertheless, sir knight, of love, thou speakest very honestly and fairly, and ye hold love in great worship, as is plain to see, and so at last ye shall doubtless receive the high guerdon and reward of that lord Love whose lauds and offices ye so well recite." And then that fair lady looked on Sir Lancelot with right good liking. And as they passed on their way they came to a lake, and all about it there were yew-trees set as a high hedge, and from the shadow of these trees they heard issuing a noise of lamentation. "What is this?" said Guinevere. "Let us delay and listen." And there was a sound of a man who wept, and after his weeping they saw him take a lute, and he sang this melody:

I make an incantation against the brightness of the sky:
I make an incantation against the shining of the sun:
I make an incantation against the wind of heaven.

I utter a spell against the boughs of the oak,
Against the aspen, and the alder, the willow and the birch,
Against the budding of every tree that is in the wood.

I bind a charm against the rose that it blossom not:
May my magic bring darkness on the generation of the flowers:
May blackness consume the grass of the fields.

Let there be a mighty spell upon the melody of the birds,
Let the green perpetual choir be silent,
Let the song of fairyland be heard no more.
For in Gwenllian was the brightness of the sky,
She was the splendour of the heavenly sun,
She imparted sweetness to the breeze from on high.
In her were contained the delight of the woods,
The sweetness of the rose, the pleasure of the flowers.
Her voice gave rapture to the song of the birds.
The joys of the world have departed with her to Paradise.

And Guinevere and Sir Lancelot went on their way considering the sad estate of this desolate lover, and again the lady spoke and said: 'What say ye, sir knight? Will ye still be so hardy as to praise this love that bringeth men into so piteous a case? Heard ye not how he spoke, saying that all joys had departed with that lady that death has taken from him?" "Lady," said he, "there shall come a day when ye shall understand well that, albeit lovers may die and perish, yet love remaineth ever immortal, since no pangs of death may ever assail him." And a second time Guinevere looked gently on Sir Lancelot, and in her heart she had him in right good liking.

How They Came to Camelot

After this fashion Sir Lancelot and Queen Guinevere passed through the regions of Britain, till they drew, near to Camelot, where King Arthur held his court with his Knights of the Round Table. And as they paced through the Forest of Dendreath they could see through the boughs of the trees the open country shining before them, and Sir Lancelot said: "Lady, in a day's journey we shall come to Camelot, and there shall we find King Arthur and all his Knights of the Round Table, and the ladies of his court, and the saint that shall make you King Arthur's queen." And she knew not what she should have said to this, and her heart grew sad: and then she bethought her of an old tale and matter of wizardry, or so men say. And she gazed at the trees of the wood, searching for a tree that she knew of; and as they came to the wood's verge she saw her desire, and broke off a little bough from a wych-elm that grew by the way. Then she has broken this bough in twain, and one she has hidden about her, and the other she has given to the knight, saying: "I wit well that all of my lord's knights are men of truth and gentle dealing, and I think that of them all ye be not the least. Wherefore, whatsoever ye swear to me, sure am I that ye will perform your oath and keep it, and never gainsay it not so long as ye live." "Ye say rightly, lady. What will ye that I swear to you?" "I will have ye swear that evermore while ye be quick and in this life ye keep this bough that I give you, for to be a token of this wayfaring and of my wedding of my lord, King Arthur." "So shall it be, very willingly," and Lancelot swore this by holy rood. Then at the end of their way they came to high Camelot, the golden and glorious city of King Arthur, and by the high saint were King Arthur and the Lady Guinevere made man and wife.

The Caldron of Incantation

There was a day when Queen Guinevere, that now is married to King Arthur, sat with her ladies in her bower, and they were at sport, devising of certain flowers, that were their lovers, and of their divers properties. Said one damosel: "I know a rose-tree that rises not too tall, and it grows in a low garden, and four shining waters are about this garden, and five lions keep watch over this garden, and six thorns there be on this rose-tree, and one blossom only. Tell me where my rose is hidden." Then, by computing of numbers, the other ladies made out the name of a knight and spoke it, and they all laughed with glee; and so sped their sport very merrily. But all the while the Queen sat silent, and she looked out of the window of the high tower, and saw far away the green trees in the wood, and the road by which she had passed from Cameliard to Camelot. And whereas her ladies spoke of flowers and of the knights their lovers, so her thoughts fell on the bough of the wych elm which she had broken with Lancelot; and fervently did she desire the love of this knight in her heart. Then did she wholly burn, then did her heart become as a coal of fire, and forthwith she went apart and wrote a scroll, and sent the writing to one that dwelt in Camelot, being a man reputed a sorcerer and a great clerk in art magic. So it fell out that Guinevere stole away in the night-time, and came to a hidden place in a wood that was near to Camelot, and there the wizard had ready his caldron of sorcery and incantation. And he had made set about this caldron a ring of fires, and a shining smoke went up from the vessel as it were quick glass, and within the ring you might see divers puppets and images in wax and in wood, shamefully devised and foully wrought, having on their fore heads and their breasts the signs and marks of the devils of hell and of the cursed gods and goddesses of heathen men. And with the wizard there was a lad that all the while made the fires to burn with spices and gums of Satan, and a black smoke rose up from these flames. Then came the Queen into the ring, and at the wizard's bidding she doffed all her clothes and stood naked by the caldron; and so she dipped the elm wand into the bubbling of the caldron, right as the wizard commanded her. Forthwith ye might hear a noise and a rushing sound amongst the black branches and thickets of the wood, the great boughs of the trees tossed one on other, and said the wizard: "Now, madam, the Hosts of the Air draw near; now is at hand the Army of Tzabaoth." Then, in the shimmering and in the shining of the glassy smoke that rose from the caldron there showed the shapes of the Mighty Ones, and to the Mightiest did Guinevere there make offering of herself; and, this done, "Now," said the wizard, "is the time come." Then drew forth Queen Guinevere the wych-bough from its place, and again dipped it down three times into the caldron of incantation and drew it forth, saying:

> One was one in the wood
> On the tree of old enchantment;
> One was made twain in the wood,
> A word of wisdom was uttered.
> Now, one calleth to one,
> One tree cannot be dissevered.
> By the sign of union
> Let the parted be joined together.

Then, with the great word of incantation, the lady made the sign, and forth came flying in the air Sir Lancelot, in his ghostly body. And from that night Sir Lancelot, that was the flower and crown of all King Arthur's warriors, durst not deny the Queen Guinevere in anything, but loved her from that time forth.

Mist and Mystery

The Joys of Camelot

Now at that time it is to be understood that Camelot was the wonder and prize of all the cities in the Isle of Britain, nay, of the whole world. For, like that city of Syon, it was set on a high hill, and encompassed on every side by rich gardens and bowers of delight and orchards and pleasure-places. And on high were, the palaces of the warriors and the choirs and altars of the saints, and the most lordly palace of the Emperor Arthur, as it were a mountain on a mountain. And here were assembled all the rarities and precious things of the whole world, and all the instruments of wisdom, and all the books in which the secret things were written, which Merlin had gathered together from all the coasts of the world. In this city, therefore, did Sir Lancelot and the Queen have their pleasure and delight and dalliance, and by art magic no eye could discern their pleasures, while they lived in wantonness. And ever Sir Lancelot, that was a loyal knight in his heart, must grieve and mourn for his piteous transgression against his lord, and ever must he weep and lament in his chamber for this mortal sin, and ever must he strive that it be put from him. Yet, by virtue of the spell and by the caldron of incantation, he was without succour and relief, and what the Queen would that must he do. And it fell out that one night he strove against the word of incantation and magic, and it was as if his heart was bursten within him, and down fell he on the floor of his chamber, as though he were stark dead. Then came his squire, and to him it seemed that the spirit was departed from Sir Lancelot, and he made a lamentable crying, and still Sir Lancelot lay there like a dead man. And when the life returned to him he that was the mightiest of all King Arthur's Knights of the Round Table was, as it were, a little child, and no strength, nor virtue was there left in his body. And while he lay there, there came without his window one of Guinevere's damsels, taught by the Queen, and thus she sang to him:

All through the nightertale I longed for thee,
In loneliness, and hearkened for the door
To open, or a footstep on the floor.

O lief sweetheart, I pray thee pity me,
I hunger for thy kisses evermore;
All through the nightertale I longed for thee.

Delight is turned to woe, and misery
Is my solace, certes, my heart is sore.
Yet these poor lips a smile at morning bore,
Though all the nightertale I longed for thee.

Wherefore henceforth Sir Lancelot strove no more, but lived deliciously in the golden meshes of the Queen's desires. And so to them twain the fruits of the orchards of Camelot were as apples of Avalon and golden delights, and the gardens were as walks of Paradise, and the feasts in King Arthur's hall were like the perpetual entertainment of the Blessed and Venerable Head of Brân Vendigeid, and the singing of the birds was as the song of the Three Fairy Birds of Rhiannon.

Concerning the Vision of the Sangraal

And one year King Arthur kept the feast of Pentecost at Camelot, as his custom was for the most part, and thirteen churches were set apart wherein King Arthur and his court heard mass. And afterwards, when they were in hall, suddenly there fell a silence, and each man looked on other and was afraid. Then there was a noise like thunder, and the roof was all afire; and then they heard in that place a melody as of the choirs of Paradise and the rejoicing of the angels, and ye would have said that there was an odour in that hall as of all the spicery of the world. And all the knights fell down on their knees together, and they saw as it were a hand pass from one end of the hall to the other and go forth; and the hand bore up the holy and blessed Vessel of the Sangraal, wrapt about in veils of red samite, and there was a shining of light that made the sun darkness; and to Sir Lancelot, because of his deadly sin, it was as if a sword had pierced his body, for his flesh began to tremble when he beheld the spiritual things. Yet he might not put his sin from him, but ever again returned to his dalliance with the Queen, for the spell that she had set upon him could not yet be broken.

How This Matter Ended

Now, with the passing of the years, it happened that the bough of wych-elm that Queen Guinevere had severed in the wood withered and shrank, and, though the Queen and Sir Lancelot might keep each their portion never so well, the leaves that were on the boughs fell off. And when a leaf fell off then it vanished away, and as it vanished there flew forth a great bird, black as a coal; and these birds perched on the trees of the wood, and cried out as men passed by, "Guinevere is the leman of Sir Lancelot." And so this sin could no longer be covered, and all the court of King Arthur had knowledge of these birds and of what their message was, and some believed it and some not, but all looked strangely on Sir Lancelot and Queen Guinevere. And it fell out at last that Guinevere took out her portion of the bough and set it before her, counting the leaves that remained; and suddenly she must go forth from her chamber to sit in hall; and by ill chance she has forgotten the bough, so that one of her damsels cometh in, and seeing it, casteth it into the fire. And in that moment was Sir Lancelot set free from the virtue of the enchantment and the wizardry that had been done upon him; and in that moment came the lad that had prepared the fires of the sorcery, and confessed all to the King, and the report of this was made known to all the city of Camelot. Then the anger of King Arthur was like to burning of fire, and he sent ten knights, that were the mightiest that he had, to waylay Sir Lancelot, that they might slay him forthwith and hew his body in pieces. So these knights went forth, and they came upon Sir Lancelot as he walked in his garden, and he had no arms, but only a short sword, upon him. Then they cried: "Now shall ye surely die, thou foul and disloyal knight, for the deep dishonour that ye have done our lord the King," and they ran at him to kill him. But, for all their mail, five of them did he leave for dead in that garden, since he was the most valorous and most mightiest of all knights that ever have been in this world; and so the five knights that were left in life fled away from before Sir Lancelot. Then would Sir Lancelot endeavour to bring forth the Queen harmless, but he might not, she was so closely kept; and so Sir Lancelot fled forth from Camelot, and gathered his kinsfolk about him, if haply he might, deliver the Queen from prison. For Arthur swore that for wizardry and disloyalty she should be burnt. But afterward King Arthur repented of his oath, and Guinevere dwelt, as all men know, in an abbey of nuns at Amesbury, and in due time was Sir Lancelot hallowed Bishop of Canterbury. And so, having repented of their sins, they both departed from this life; on whose souls may God have pity.

OUT OF THE EARTH.

By ARTHUR MACHEN, Author of " The Bowmen."

I

There was some sort of confused complaint during last August of the ill-behaviour of the children at certain Welsh watering places. Such reports and vague rumours are most difficult to trace to their heads and fountains; none has better reason to know that than myself. I need not go over the old ground here, but I am afraid that many people are wishing by this time that they had never heard my name; again, a considerable number of estimable persons are concerning themselves gloomily enough, from my point of view, with my everlasting welfare. They write me letters, some in kindly remonstrance, begging me not to deprive poor sick-hearted souls of what little comfort they possess amidst their sorrows. Others send me tracts and pink leaflets with allusions to "the daughter of a well-known canon"; others again are violently and anonymously abusive. And then in open print, in fair book-form, Mr. Begbie has dealt with me righteously but harshly, as I cannot but think.

II

Yet, it was all so entirely innocent, nay casual, on my part. A poor linnet of prose, I did but perform my indifferent piping in the "Evening News" because I wanted to do so, because I felt that the story of "The Bowmen" ought to be told. An inventor of fantasies is a poor creature, heaven knows, when all the world is at war; but I thought that no harm would be done, at any rate, if I bore witness, after the fashion of the fantastic craft, to my belief in the heroic glory of the English host who went back from Mons fighting and triumphing.

III

And then, somehow or other, it was as if I had touched a button and set in action a terrific, complicated mechanism of rumours that pretended to be sworn truth, of gossips that posed as evidence, of wild tarradiddles that good men most firmly believed. The supposed testimony of that "daughter of a well-known canon" took parish magazines by storm, and equally enjoyed the faith of dissenting divines. The "daughter" denied all knowledge of the matter, but people still quoted her supposed sure word; and the issues were confused with tales, probably true, of painful hallucinations and deliriums of our retreating soldiers, men fatigued and shattered to the very verge of death. It all became worse than the Russian myths, and as in the fable of the Russians, it seemed impossible to follow the streams of delusion to their fountain-head—or heads. Who was it who said that "Miss M. knew two officers who, etc., etc.?" I suppose we shall never know his lying, deluding name.

IV

And so, I dare say, it will be with this strange affair of the troublesome children of the Welsh seaside town, or rather of a group of small towns and villages lying within a certain "section" or zone, which I am not going to indicate more precisely than I can help, since I love that country, and my recent experiences with "The Bowmen" have taught me that no tale is too idle to be believed. And, of course, to begin with, nobody knew how this odd and malicious piece of gossip originated. So far as I know, it was more akin to the Russian myth than to the tale of "The Angels of Mons." That is, rumour preceded print; the thing was talked of here and there and passed from letter to letter long before the papers were aware of its existence. And—here it resembles, rather the Mons affair—London and Manchester, Leeds and Birmingham were muttering vague unpleasant things while the little villages concerned basked innocently in the sunshine of an unusual prosperity.

V

In this last circumstance, as some believe, is to be sought the root of the whole matter. It is well known that certain east-coast towns suffered from the dread of air-raids, and that a good many of their usual visitors went westward for the first time. So there is a theory that the East Coast was mean enough to circulate reports against the West Coast out of pure malice and envy. It may be so; I do not pretend to know. But here is a personal experience, such as it is, which illustrates the way in which the rumour was circulated. I was lunching one day at my Fleet Street tavern—this was early in July—and a friend of mine, a solicitor, of Serjeants' Inn, came in and sat at the same table. We began to talk of holidays and my friend Eddis asked me where I was going. "To the same old place," I said. "Manavon. You know we always go there." "Are you really?" said the lawyer; "I thought that coast had gone off a lot. My wife has a friend who's heard that it's not at all what it was."

VI

I was astonished to hear this, not seeing how a little village like Manavon could have "gone off." I had known it for ten years as having accommodation for about twenty visitors, and I could not believe that rows of lodging houses had sprung up since the August of 1914. Still I put the question to Eddis: "Trippers?" I asked, knowing firstly that trippers hate the solitudes of the country and the sea; secondly, that there are no industrial towns within cheap and easy distance; and thirdly, that the railways were issuing no excursion tickets during the war.

"No, not exactly trippers," the lawyer replied. "But my wife's friend knows a clergyman who says that the beach at Tremaen is not at all pleasant now, and Tremaen's only a few miles from Manavon, isn't it?"

"In what way not pleasant?" I carried on my examination. "Pierrots and shows, and that sort of thing?" I felt that it could not be so, for the solemn rocks of Tremaen would have turned the liveliest Pierrot to stone. He would have frozen into a crag on the beach, and the seagulls would carry away his song and make it a lament by lonely booming caverns that look on Avalon. Eddis said he had heard nothing about showmen; but he understood that since the war the children of the whole district had got quite out of hand.

"Bad language, you know," he said, "and all that sort of thing, worse than London slum children. One doesn't want one's wife and children to hear foul talk at any time, much less on their holiday. And they say that Castell Coch is quite impossible; no decent woman would be seen there!"

I said: "Really, that's a great pity," and changed the subject. But I could not make it out at all. I knew Castell Coch well—a little bay bastioned by the dunes of red sandstone cliffs, rich with greenery. A stream of cold water runs down there to the sea; there is the ruined Norman Castle, the ancient church and the scattered village; it is altogether a place of peace and quiet and great beauty. The people there, children and grown-ups alike, were not merely decent but courteous folk: if one thanked a child for opening a gate, there would come the inevitable response: "And welcome kindly, sir." I could not make it out at all. I didn't believe the lawyer's tales; for the life of me I could not see what he could be driving at. And, for the avoidance of all unnecessary mystery, I may as well say that my wife and child and myself went down to Manavon last August and had a most delightful holiday. At the time we were certainly conscious of no annoyance or unpleasantness of any kind. Afterwards, I confess, I heard a story that puzzled and still puzzles me, and this story, if it be received, might give its own interpretation to one or two circumstances which seemed in themselves quite insignificant.

VII

But all through July I came upon traces of evil rumours affecting this most gracious corner of the earth. Some of these rumours were repetitions of Eddis' gossip; others amplified his vague story and made it more definite. Of course, no first-hand evidence was available. There never is any first-hand evidence in these cases. But A knew B who had heard from C that her second-cousin's little girl had been set upon and beaten by a pack of young Welsh savages. Then people quoted "a doctor in large practice in a well-known town in the Midlands," to the effect that Tremaen was a sink of juvenile depravity. They said that a responsible medical man's evidence was final and convincing; but they didn't bother to find out who the doctor was, or whether there was any doctor at all—or any doctor relevant to the issue. Then the thing began to get into the papers in a sort of oblique, by-the-way sort of manner. People cited the case of these imaginary bad children in support of their educational views. One side said that "these unfortunate little ones" would have been quite well-behaved if they had had no education at all; the opposition declared that continuation schools would speedily reform them and make them into admirable citizens. Then the poor Arfonshire children seemed to become involved in quarrels about Welsh Disestablishment and in the question of the trainers; and all the while they were going about behaving politely and admirably as they always do behave. I knew all the time that it was all nonsense, but I couldn't understand in the least what it meant, or who was pulling the wires of rumour, or their purpose in so pulling. I began to wonder whether the pressure and anxiety and suspense of a terrible war had unhinged the public mind, so that it was ready to believe any fable to debate the reasons for happenings which had never happened. At last, quite incredible things began to be whispered: visitors' children had not only been beaten, they had been tortured; a little boy had been found impaled on a stake in a lonely field near Manavon; another child had been lured to destruction over the cliffs at Castell Coch. A London paper sent a good man down quietly to Arfon to investigate. He was away for a week, and at the end of that period returned to his office and, in his own phrase, "threw the whole story down." There was not a word of truth, he said, in any of these rumours; no vestige of a foundation for the mildest forms of all this gossip. He had never seen such a beautiful country; he had never met pleasanter men, women or children; there was not a single case of anyone having been annoyed or troubled in any sort or fashion.

VIII

Yet all the while the story grew, and grew more monstrous and incredible. I was too much occupied in watching the progress of my own mythological monster to pay much attention. The Town Clerk of Tremaen to which the legend had at length penetrated, wrote a brief letter to the Press indignantly denying that there was the slightest foundation for "the unsavoury rumours" which, he understood, were being circulated; and about this time we went down to Manavon and, as I say, enjoyed ourselves extremely. The weather, was perfect: blues of paradise in the skies, the seas all a shimmering wonder, olive greens and emeralds, rich purples, glassy sapphires changing by the rocks; far away a haze of magic lights and colours at the meeting of sea and sky. Work and anxiety had harried me; I found nothing better than to rest on the thymy banks by the shore, finding an infinite balm and refreshment in the great sea before me, in tiny the flowers beside me. Or we would rest all the summer afternoon on a "shelf" high on the grey cliffs and watch the tide creaming and surging about the rocks, and listen to it booming in the hollows and caverns below. Afterwards, as I say, there were one or two things that struck cold. But at the time those were nothing. You see a man in an odd white hat pass by and think little or nothing about it. Afterwards, when you hear that a man wearing just such a hat had committed murder in the next street five minutes before, then you find in that hat a certain interest and significance. "Funny children," was the phrase my little boy used; and I began to think they were "funny" indeed.

IX

If there be a key at all to this queer business, I think it is to be found in a talk I had not long ago with a friend of mine named Morgan. He is a Welshman and a dreamer, and some people say he is like a child who has grown up and yet has not grown up like other children of men. Though I did not know it, while 1 was at Manavon, he was spending his holiday time at Castell Coch. He was a lonely man and he liked lonely places, and when we met in the autumn he told me how, day after day, he would carry his bread and cheese and beer in a basket to a remote headland on that coast known as the Old Camp. Here, far above the waters, are solemn age-old walls, turf-grown; circumvallations rounded and smooth with the passing of many thousand years. At one end of this most ancient place there is a tumulus, a tower of observation, perhaps, and underneath it slinks the green deceiving ditch that seems to wind into the heart of the camp, but in reality rushes down to sheer rock and a precipice over the waters.

Here came Morgan daily, as he said, to dream of Avalon, to purge himself from the fuming corruption of the streets.

And so, as he told me, it was with singular horror that one afternoon as he dozed and dreamed and opened his eyes now and again to watch the miracle and magic of the sea, as he listened to the myriad murmurs of the waves, his meditation was broken by a sudden burst of horrible raucous cries—and the cries of children, too, but children of the lowest type. Morgan says that the very tones made him shudder—"They were to the ear what slime is to the touch," and then the words: every foulness, every filthy abomination of speech; blasphemies that struck like blows at that sky, that sank down into the pure shining depths, defiling them! He was amazed. He peered over the green wall of the fort, and there in the ditch he saw a swarm of noisome children, horrible little stunted creatures with old men's faces, with bloated faces, with little sunken eyes, with leering eyes. It was worse than uncovering a brood of snakes or a nest of worms.

No; he would not describe what they were about. "Read about Belgium," said Morgan, "and think they couldn't have been more than five or six years old." There was no infamy, he said, that they did not perpetrate; they spared no horror of cruelty. "I saw blood running in streams, as they shrieked with laughter, but I could not find the mark of it on the grass afterwards."

Morgan said he watched them and could not utter a word; it was as if a hand held his mouth tight. But at last he found his voice and shrieked at them, and they burst into a yell of obscene laughter and shrieked back at him, and scattered out of sight. He could not trace them; he supposes that they hid in the deep bracken behind the Old Camp.

"Sometimes I can't understand my landlord at Castell Coch,"

Morgan went on. "He's the village postmaster and has a little farm of his own—a decent, pleasant, ordinary sort of chap. But now and again he will talk oddly. I was telling him about these beastly children and wondering, who, they could he when he broke into Welsh, something like 'the battle that is for age unto ages; and the people take delight in it.'"

X

So far Morgan, and it was evident that he did not understand at all. But this strange tale of his brought back an odd circumstance or two that I recollected: a matter of our little boy straying away more than once, and getting lost among the sand dunes and coming back screaming, evidently frightened horribly, and babbling about "funny children." We took no notice; did not trouble, I think, to look whether there were any children wandering about the dunes or not. We were accustomed to his small imaginations.

But after hearing Morgan's story I was interested, and I wrote an account of the matter to my friend, old Doctor Duthoit, of Hereford. And he:

"They were only visible, only audible to children and the childlike. Hence the explanation of what puzzled you at first; the rumours, how did they arise? They arose from nursery gossip, from scraps and odds and ends of half-articulate children's talk of horrors that they didn't understand, of words that shamed their nurses and their mothers.

"These little people of the earth rise up and rejoice in these times of ours. For they are glad, as the Welshman said, when they know that men follow their walks."

Part Two

Articles and Reviews

THE OCCULT WORLD.

There is a singular article in the March number of the "Occult Review." It is called "Goethe as an Occultist," and the writer, Mr. A. S. Furnell, gives his reasons for bestowing the title of "occultist" on the great German poet. To begin with, his grandfather was possessed of the prophetic faculty.

This gentleman, Goethe relates, while still in an inferior municipal post, assured his wife that the lot would fall on him to be alderman at the next vacancy. He had seen himself in a dream in the assembly of town councillors, one of whom rose up, offered him his place, and left the room. Shortly after, the alderman thus dreamt of died, and the lot fell on Goethe's grandfather, as he had predicted.

Now, I see no reason whatever for disbelieving this story. It may be true, it may be untrue; but to the best of my belief human history is full of similar instances, as well authenticated as any incident can be. I believe that there can be no doubt as to the story of the Cornishman who dreamed that he saw Perceval, the Prime Minister, assassinated, and asked his neighbours whether he would do well to go up to London to warn the victim. There are scores and hundreds of similar instances. My own grandmother was warned in a dream not to let her daughter visit a certain house; and the very night that house and all in it were overwhelmed by a great flood. And I do not think that telepathy can be adduced as an explanation of all these cases. The assassin's mind might have communicated its intent to the Cornishman; but the terrific storm of rain which burst the cisterns of the Breconshire hills could not have been in the foreknowledge of any human being. The dream of Goethe's grandfather, to be sure, is not highly evidential; it may, very possibly, have been suggested by desire.

However, we will waive this objection, and allow the existence of the prophetic dream.

Equally, I have no objection to make against some "psychic" experiences of the great poet himself. Goethe, it is here related, visited the battlefield of Jena, on a "psychical research" expedition.

> On a certain hill under which many French soldiers were buried both saw a figure striding slowly up and down. . . . Goethe's breath came with difficulty. "Truly a French soldier," he murmured. We were quite near, about twenty paces from it. . . . We recognised it distinctly, the high boots, white trousers, the coat with shoulder-belt, and the high cap.

Well, Goethe challenged the soldier without result; shot at him, and still the soldier walked on; rushed at him—and found there was nothing. It may have been so; I do not know anything about "Geheimrat K——," or whether the Geheimrat's word is to be trusted. The same witness tells how Goethe saw in the midst of an empty road his friend "Friedrich," habited in the poet's own dressing-gown and slippers. Goethe feared that "Friedrich" must be dead, but on reaching his house the spectral gentleman was discovered on Goethe's sofa, clothed in the costume of the vision. Perhaps so; and what then?

Well, I think the rational response to the message of such facts as we are considering is twofold. In the first place, if we are so unfortunate as to have been materialists, we must confess that the materialistic hypothesis is disproved. And, secondly, if we are tolerably intelligent, we must confess also that the "psychic experience" is, ultimately, of very little consequence. The true spiritual life, the true mystic life, the true intellectual life are utterly independent of the dreams of Goethe's grandfather as to the aldermanic chair awaiting him. One might as well propose that London should be lighted by "ignes fatui" or will-o'-the-wisps, in place of incandescent gas and electricity, as attempt to build up a church and feed one's soul on a spectral "Friedrich" in dressing-gown and slippers on the high road.

But on the other hand there is the way of the "Occult Review." Once convinced that the eidolon of "Friedrich," of dressing-gown and slippers, was really seen by Goethe, the "occultist'" says "ergo gluc," which, being interpreted, means: "Therefore every crazy dogma which has something of the marvellous about it is true. If a man tells me that he can conjure up the spirit of my great aunt for £1 1s., I will believe him; if another man says that he can get me the 'telescript' of Shakespeare for 10s. 6d., I will believe him also. If Dr. Franz Hartmann declares that a book perfectly well known at the British Museum was given to him by a Rosicrucian abbot in a Himalayan monastery, that will I hold as true. When 'mediums' are caught flagrante delicto, loudly will I assert that this is to me the crowning proof of 'spiritualism.' Especially will I cherish every sort of gibberish, ancient and modern, as infinitely more exalted than the Christian Faith. Convicted impostors such as Blavatsky I will place on a pinnacle high above St. John the Divine, and criminals of a disgusting kind, wanted by the police, shall be my apostles and evangelists. 'Letters from Julia' shall lie under my pillow, and from my heart I confess that trick artists from 'the halls' do their tricks by the aid of many ghosts. And when Mrs. Tomson comes out of the cabinet in white tulle, then will I recognise a departed relative. All imposture have I taken for my province, and every marvel will I believe—if only it be not contained in the Gospels." Such is the way of the modern occultist.

To the Editor of T.P.'s WEEKLY.

Sir,—I notice on page 364 of your issue of March 19 certain statements by a correspondent who signs himself "M." As these totally misrepresent the entire attitude taken up by my magazine, I must ask permission to occupy some of your valuable space for their exposure. The cause of the attack is an article of a very temperate and logical character, entitled "Goethe as an Occultist." This article, which is so evidential and non-committal in its character that it might well have appeared in any ordinary

London monthly periodical, is made the text of a tirade against the "Occult Review" for accepting facts in the region of the super-normal regardless of their possibility or the scientific evidence in support of them. Your contributor, in some remarks which do not give the ordinary reader a very high impression of his intelligence, commences by stating that because Goethe saw an "eidolon" of a friend in dressing-gown and slippers, that therefore the occultist says "Ergo gluc," which he is good enough to interpret, as meaning "therefore every crazy dogma which has something of the marvellous about it is true." I think there are few of the readers of your paper, who will not be grateful to "M," for kindly giving a translation of these two curious words. If he had added the language from which they are taken, with which he is evidently familiar, he would have done your readers a further service. The first word doubtless suggests Latin, but as the second could by no possibility belong to this language, and is not even to be found in Du Cange's celebrated glossary, this supposition must be dismissed.

He then proceeds to give seven instances of views adopted and held by the "occultist" as illustrative of what he calls "the way of the 'Occult Review.'" As far as I am able to check them, these instances from which your contributor deduces his opinion of the magazine are not, in any single instance, to be met with in any of its pages. They are, in short, the mere fabrications of one who does not read the "Review," and who is consequently ignorant of the scientific attitude it adopts. In these circumstances it will be sufficient for me to notice one only. The "occultist"—that is, as the context conclusively shows, the Editor of the "Occult Review" (for without this assumption the whole argument would, ipso facto, fall to the ground, and the comments made be reduced to sheer nonsense)—places, we are told, "impostors such as Blavatsky on a pinnacle high above St. John the Divine!" Now, sir, I am forwarding for your inspection a copy of the issue of the "Occult Review" for February, 1906, in which the editor's opinion of the lady in question is clearly and definitely expressed, which I will ask you to be good enough to reproduce so that your readers may be in a position to judge of the amount of credibility to be attached to the other statements of your contributor. Men of eminence like Professor Alfred Russel Wallace and Professor W. F. Barrett, and others, would hardly have written in the warm terms of compliment and approval that they have done on various occasions, on the character of the magazine, had there been the least tittle or shred of truth in your contributor's statements. Nor, I would add, could the magazine have attained the high reputation and position it now enjoys had there been any justification for "M.'s" assertions. I cannot but think that it is an extremely regrettable fact that a magazine of the standing of T.P.'s WEEKLY has given currency to such a gross misrepresentation.—Yours truly,

RALPH SHIRLEY,

Editor of the "Occult Review"

Reply from Arthur Machen

[I am extremely sorry to see, by the above letter, that I have mystified, grieved, and misled Mr. Ralph Shirley, the editor of the "Occult Review." I will deal first with the mystification. Mr. Ralph Shirley does not understand what is meant by the phrase "ergo gluc." With considerable acuteness and some learning he deduces, tentatively, a Latin source for "ergo," and I am glad to confirm him in his conjecture. "Gluc " is more obscure, I confess; still, I do not think that I can fairly be held responsible for Mr. Ralph Shirley's ignorance of Rabelais—a great writer, though not more of an "occultist" than Goethe. The whole phrase may be taken to mean "ergo fol-de-rol," or, in the vulgar tongue: "therefore stuff and nonsense." Secondly, as for Mr. Shirley's grievances, I do not agree with him that the article on "Goethe" was at all evidential. I should call it, for the most part, mere hearsay, and I think that in any court of justice what "Geheimrat K——" said would share the fate of what, the soldier said (Bardell v. Pickwick, Stareleigh J.).

The next point is a more serious one: The Editor of the "Occult Review" assumes that by "the occultist" I meant himself. He is not warranted in making any such assumption. My English, I trust, is clear; and I refer him to the plain words of my article. If Mr. Shirley chooses to identify himself with "the occultist"—of course I cannot prevent his doing so, but neither can I admit that such identification is indispensable to my argument. As to the authority attributed by large numbers of occultists to "H. P. B.," as compared with St. John the Divine, the writings and the speeches of prominent Theosophists will give Mr. Shirley sufficient information on that point. I have read the copy of the "Occult Review" for February, 1906, in which the Editor, recording the death of Dr. Hodgson, mentions him as "the exposer of the Blavatsky frauds," and gives Dr. Hodgson's conclusions as to Madame Blavatsky's "trick cabinets," &c., &c. I would remind Mr. Shirley again that was speaking of "occultists" in general, amongst whom Theosophists are included, and by these occultists the report of the Psychical Research Committee, was, called "H. P. B.'s 'Calvary'"—which suggests that the occult theory of comparative values is sufficiently audacious. I must decline to discuss with Mr. Ralph Shirley the "high reputation and position" which, as he says, his magazine now enjoys.— M.]

The Occult World. To the Editor of T.P.'s WEEKLY.

Sir,—I have read with interest the communication of "M." in reply to my repudiation of his attack upon the "Occult Review," and, in view of its nature, there is now little left for me but to dot the "i's" and cross the "t's " of this remarkable document.

The attack which he made was either based on the seven charges previously referred to, or, alternatively, it was entirely baseless—a mere outburst of spleen on the part of the writer. I now learn from his own pen that these charges, following and apparently intended to support his attack upon the "Occult Review," had, in fact, nothing whatever to do with the matter, just as one might say, "What fine weather we are having," or some equally irrelevant remark. He thus pleads guilty to an anonymous and slanderous attack, which, by his own showing, he has made no sort of attempt to justify.

Surely, this disciple of Rabelais, and "St. John the Divine" should have known better manners.

The fact is, the "Way of the 'Occult Review" is the way of Evidence, and the "way" of your contributor "M.," though apparently he has not the courage to admit it, is the way of Tradition—that is, the way of all the "N.'s" and "M.'s" who, from time immemorial, have subscribed automatically to the effete and out-worn catechisms of the past. The two standpoints are like Kipling's East and West, "and never the twain shall meet."—I am, Sir, yours faithfully,

RALPH SHIRLEY.

Reply from Arthur Machen

[I note, with regret, the particular horn of the dilemma on which Mr. Ralph Shirley has chosen to impale himself. For his letter makes it plain that he has fitted on his head the cap of occultism; that he does regard himself as a representative of the "occultist" of my article. I do not plead guilty to any offence of any kind or sort; it is Mr. Shirley who, of his own free will, ranges himself with this tragical-comical host of deceivers and deceived. It is quite clear that Mr. Shirley is a disciple neither of St. John nor of Rabelais; I wish I could think that he was at least a disciple of William of Wykeham.—M.]

THE CHURCH PAGEANT: A MORALITY.

I am devoutly thankful that it is not my task to write a thorough and detailed criticism of the great Church Pageant at Fulham. I am neither an expert in ecclesiastical and English history, nor an expert in ancient music, nor an expert in mediæval, Celtic, and Roman costume, nor an expert in ecclesiology; and all these expert voices would have to be united into one before a competent notice of the pageant could be written. We have heard a good deal during the last week or so as to the admirable accomplishments of the modern journalist, so I have no doubt that the ideal criticism has appeared, or will appear shortly. There is only one thing that I must say, and that is that I have never seen so fine an example of stage management and grouping as that displayed by Mr. Hugh Moss, the Master of the Pageant. Edgar Poe maintained that landscape gardening was a fine art; if that be true, then we must reckon amongst the fine arts the glowing and changing and shining mosaics of colour that Mr. Moss has created under the trees at Fulham.

But, all criticism apart, the pageantry has, I think, certain suggestions and morals. And the first of these moral headlines I will make bold to convey from Mr. G. K. Chesterton, who said long ago that Paganism only survives in Christianity. Indeed, I do not know whether I am right to credit Mr. Chesterton with the invention of this paradox, for I remember that something of the kind, put from a different standpoint, used to be one of the commonplaces of a certain school of Christian controversialists. These worthy and earnest persons protested against flowers because flowers were used in Pagan worship; they were for extinguishing lights because the heathen had lit them, and vestments, said they, were fit only for the congregations of Jove and the chapelries of Venus. Well, I believe that a very different school has carried this line of thought a little farther; has shown, or has attempted to show, that Christianity owes somewhat more than its external decorations to the former times and to the gods of older days. And, at all events, the line of argument which says "This, that, and the other are pagan, and therefore abominable" is a dangerous one, leading to all sorts of odd consequences. But Mr. Chesterton, of course, was appealing to an audience of a very different kind; he was speaking to those who have embraced the opposite heresy of "Pagan, therefore beautiful"—nonsense also—and he tells his unchristian young friends that if they would be really good Pagans they must certainly go to church! And the pageant demonstrated the plain truth of Mr. Chesterton's paradox. One saw the old natural worship, purged and moralised and transmuted, rise before one as the pomp of the Churchmen went by in its fervent and admirable order. Before them young men in pure white robes carried the mystic insignia and symbols of the Faith, more especially the Symbol of the Great Paradox, whereby the world—always at heart in love with brute force, and applause of men, and an evident success, and a big balance at the bank—is instructed that the most shameful defeat was the most shining of all victories. Then, beside this ensign, the burning torches spoke of an internal light, brighter than that of the sun; and the incense fuming from the golden censer demonstrated that odour has its full claim to discourse of hidden mysteries. And the vestments of the priests, of cloth of gold and of divers colours, had their recondite significance for the initiated, but spoke to all of splendours which have nothing in common with luxuries, of fine raiment which has ceased to be a handsome dress, having been changed into a symbol, a hieroglyphic of eternal mysteries of love and redemption. The folk-lore students tell us, I think, that in certain tribes of savages the earliest clothes *were* vestments, so that perhaps our neat business suits in blue serge or black cloth at 49s. 6d. for cash may be in a sense the descendants of the sacrificial robes of some awful and primæval ritual. However that may be, those who sat and watched at Fulham saw that such common things as clothes, which we use to keep ourselves warm, to keep ourselves vain, and to spite our neighbours, are patient of a magic consecration, may be assumed into the region of the mysteries. And as the procession of pure white and gleaming gold, with burning tapers and smoking incense, passed on its way, there rose from it the incantation of the old Church song, in strange and awful modulations, aspiring into that heaven to which rise the springing pinnacles of the great cathedrals. Let me then play clerk to Mr. Chesterton's parson—the metaphor is ecclesiastical, and well-suited to the matter of this discourse—and entreat all true devotees of Greek antiquity to frequent the places of these mysteries; at all events during the present distress, and pending the restoration of the authentic worship of the Cyprian goddess. In these days the veritable rite of Roses and Raptures is not celebrated; let the worshippers of the Paphian make the best they can of the "substituted word" of the Christian Liturgy.

Then there is another commonplace reflection, arising to a certain extent from what has been said, but more general in its application. We have seen how the spectators of the pageant beheld a sight which was, in its sum, a beautiful work of art, and we have seen, too, that this masterpiece was composed of things common and material and sensible. Here were strips of stuff that we may buy in the shops—blue and green, purple and scarlet, white and dusky, grey and yellow and golden; here were lighted candles and spices burning in brass pots; here were certain sequences of sound; here bits of wood nailed cross wise. The matter, it will be seen, is ordinary enough, and it seems to me that one has here a statement of the mystery of all art, and eventually of all life. From the point of view of science, of materialism; what is Westminster Abbey but a heavy heap of stones; what are the masterpieces of painting save pigments on canvas? Homer made his Odyssey out of the words used in buying garlic and goats' meat, in greeting friends and in cursing enemies. A pageant, and a poem, and a picture, and a cathedral, and life itself—all these are made of common things, of the coarse matter of the universe. The stone lies bedded in the quarry, rough, shapeless, without form, and void of meaning or beauty; it is the work of the artist to utter the great word of transmutation, to say, in the phrase of Robert Fludd: "Be ye changed, be ye changed from dead stones to living and alchemical stones."[1] And so with life: there is red stuff in it, and grey stuff, and blacks for mourning, and gold for joy, and pebbles that by attrition and contrition shine gloriously, and odours of bruised and burning desires, and sounds of sorrow and gladness. All these rude elements, surely, it is our business to conjure and transmute, quickening the dead, changing dust into the stars, bringing disorder and rude chaos into a fair pattern and order. It is as we please: life may be an ugly and noisome and squalid struggle—an affair of a raging mob, going this way and that, hungering and thirsting, and slaying and trampling, without end or purpose; or else it may become cosmic, a splendid and ordered pageant, in which the grey is as necessary as the scarlet, and gold leads to the celestial azure.

Then there is the final morality, which takes the form of a question. It is this: Were the Middle Ages really the Dark Ages; or, was the "ethos" in our forefathers which lived up to the time of Henry VIII. so wholly bad as some of us have supposed? During these "dark ages" there was a certain ecclesiastical system, a certain political system, and a certain economic system. Were all these systems wholly and entirely wrong? Macauley would not have hesitated to say "Yes; decidedly and utterly wrong." Can we assent? Can we say that we have, in every region of thought and action, advanced from darkness to light? Surely not, if the maxim that the tree is known by its fruit is to hold good. Lincoln Cathedral was not built by black-hearted and brutish barbarians; the "Morte d'Arthur," and the "Divine Comedy," and the "Don Quixote" were not penned by besotted imbeciles; Crecy, Poitiers, and Agincourt were not won by downtrodden slaves. It is true that we have invented margarine, and that Manchester is, in the main, a modern town.

---

1 Robertus de Fluctibus (1574-1637) was an alchemist and physician who famously debated Johannes Kepler.

THE MASTER MYSTERY.

There is a very old and well-worn "tag" in the Latin tongue. Its meaning is: People want to be taken in; well, let them be taken in. And I don't think that I ever saw a more perfect illustration of this saying than the account of an "amazing séance" reported in the paper a week or so ago. The circumstances were as follows:—Mr. and Mrs. Clarence Thomson,[1] who have been giving a performance called "The Master Mystery" at the Alhambra Music Hall, were taken to a private house in Park Square, Regent's Park, where, under the direction of Dr. Wallace,[2] Mr. W. T. Stead,[3] a couple of Oxford professors, some medical men, and several members of the Society for Psychical Research, they were undressed and examined, dressed again in other people's clothes, and conducted to a cabinet provided by Mr. Stead. Mrs. Thomson sat inside the cabinet; Mr. Thomson sat outside the cabinet, "some yards away." All lights, except a red lamp were extinguished. Then "a figure draped in a white gauzy material appeared at the entrance of the cabinet, disappeared, and appeared again on six successive occasions—seven times in all." Four of these appearances were recognised as Mrs. Thomson; three were not. A piece of the gauze was cut off, and so far has not been matched in the West-End. Finally:

> Mr. Thomson refused to say whether spiritualism or trickery was the secret, claiming only to be a producer of mysteries. But, in a letter to him, Mr. Stead states that friends in the spirit world say that he [Mr. Thomson] does

---

1 As of the printing of this edition, the identities of Mr. and Mrs. Thomson remain elusive, but the couple were no doubt an act akin to stage magic.

2 A naturalist, explorer and spiritualist, Alfred Russel Wallace (1823-1913) was born in Llanbadoc, Monmouthshire not far from Machen's childhood home.

3 W. T. Stead (1849-1912) was an editor and spiritualist who died on the *Titanic*.

not realise the powers he possesses, and that through him they could astonish the world if he would let them.

I am told that some years ago it was gravely maintained in spiritualist circles that Mr. Maskelyne[4] ran his show at the Egyptian Hall by the aid of multitudes of the Bodiless Ones— only he hadn't the decency to acknowledge the fact.

And yet, in spite of such cases as this, in spite of hundreds of others like it, I do not think that we are justified in going to the extreme of a Universal negative. In the first place, such a position is profoundly illogical; we may say, if we like, "I have never seen a fairy," or "I don't believe in the existence of fairies," or "I intend to act on the presumption that fairies are non-existent"; but we must not say "There are no fairies," in the sense in which we say "There are no triangles with two sides." And I am rather inclined to think that Mr. Simon Newcomb,[5] the able author of "Modern Occultism" in the January number of the "Nineteenth Century," approaches perilously near to this position of universal denial.

Or, if he has not quite said in his heart that there are no ghosts, and no such things as telepathy and clairvoyance, he at least fails to state the case logically. His analogy is radium, its discovery, and its properties; and this is his conclusion:

Radio-activity is a science because it is a general fact which everyone can verify that, if you organise a certain system of experiments, you can, take a photograph through many opaque substances. That coal will burn when brought into contact with fire is a proposition belonging to the same domain. But if we could only say that someone in England had at some time made coal burn, then, a few years later, someone in Russia, then someone in America, and so on, such facts, though they mounted into the hundreds or

---

4 Nevil Maskelyne (1863-1924) was a famous stage magician of the era.

5 Simon Newcomb (1835-1909) was a Canadian-American astronomer and polymath.

the thousands, would not establish the law that coal was combustible, and therefore would not belong to science.

But, in the first place, I beg to differ from this conclusion. Such facts would establish the law that coal is sometimes combustible. There was an earthquake at Lisbon in the eighteenth century; there was another at Krakatoa more than twenty years ago; there was an earthquake at Messina last December—and such incidents establish the fact that earthquakes occasionally happen.

The other fact—that we don't know when earthquakes are going to happen—and the fact that Sir William Crookes[6] cannot produce an earthquake to order, simply show that the causes of earthquakes are to a great extent beyond our knowledge, and wholly beyond our control. And, then, I think that the whole analogy between radio-activity and what I suppose we must call "the supernatural" is bad. You can't put a ghost, supposing that such a thing exists, into a tube and look at it when you feel inclined; but that is no reason for disbelieving in ghosts. A stock breeder—taking into account a certain percentage of failures—can guarantee the production of prize beasts; but no one can guarantee the production of pedigree Dantes or black-haired Tennysons, or even of champion long-reach Ranjitsinhjis. Yet the existence of these supernormal phenomena—Dante, Tennyson, and the Indian prince—does prove that human beings are occasionally great poets and great cricketers. And then Mr. Newcomb lays stress on the law of coincidences; he inquires how many people have had premonitions, without subsequent fulfilment. This is very well, as far as it goes; but it by no means covers the whole ground. To quote two striking histories which have recently appeared in T.P.'s WEEKLY, I do not see how coincidence can produce the spectre of a red-haired girl in an empty house or the sound of heavy footfalls from void space.

---

6 William Crookes (1832-1919) was an accomplished scientist and firm beleiver in the paranormal. He is mentioned in Machen's remarkable novella, *The Great Return* (1915).

THE ENGLISH RENAISSANCE.

Mr. Laurie Magnus,[1] the author of "English Literature in the Nineteenth Century" (Melrose. 7s. 6d. net), has prescribed for himself a very difficult task, and I think that he may be congratulated on a successful achievement. This is a book which students of modern literature should buy and keep on their shelves. It gives the landmarks, the divisions, and the subdivisions of the literary field in the nineteenth century; I do not know any work, which charts the way so usefully, clearly, and intelligently. We are already well on our twentieth-century path, and the moment is well chosen to look back once more, to note the passage from Pope to Wordsworth, and to deduce, if we can, from new examples the literary future of our language.

The two names that I have just quoted are, in a sense, the key and password of the English literary renaissance, which, I believe, Mr. Watts Dunton has called the renaissance of wonder. In these two great names we have expressed the whole antinomy between two schools of literature, of art, and of thought. The school of Pope is material, the school of Wordsworth spiritual. I once showed an engraving of Botticelli's "Virgin" to a curate, and his criticism was, "It's like nothing on earth." He was evidently of the school of Pope. When Pope said that mankind was the proper study of man, he meant men as observable in St. James's or at Hampton Court, as actuated by motives intelligible to himself, and George II., and Sir Robert Walpole. Wordsworth could have echoed Pope's dictum, but he would have used the phrase in a very different sense. His great ode on the Intimations of Immortality is a study of men, just as the "Dunciad" is a study of man: the latter is particular, the former is universal. If Plato could have read these two compositions, he might have been

---

1 Dr. Laurie Magnus (1872-1933) was an English journalist and publisher.

puzzled and entertained in a slight fashion by the "Dunciad"; but he would have found in the "Ode" the utterances of a fellow countryman, of a prophet who delivered in other accents the great catholic message.

There, is, of course, no reason on earth why the two philosophies should not dwell together in perfect peace and amity. A man is a highly composite creature: in his exaltation he is Wordsworthian, doubtless, and finds his highest and most acute delights in searching the very depths of his being, in penetrating beyond the remotest bournes of time and space. But a man must dine, must laugh, must be amused; he likes to note the little peculiarities of his neighbours, he is entertained by the social traffic of his day. But the nineteenth century determined and I think very wisely, that work of this sort was best done in prose; and so Pope became Jane Austen, Thackeray, Anthony Trollope, who were able to survey mankind with all the greater ease and advantage in that they were not constrained by the limits of the heroic couplet. For poetry, as Mr. Magnus shows, is a kind of magic, a species of incantation, and its special and distinctive form is wasted and misapplied in dealing with the surfaces and obvious facets of the universe. It does not measure and weigh the crystal; it sees visions rather in its depths. It uses the sensuous to attain the spiritual, the temporal to gain the eternal. So Mr. Magnus on Coleridge's "Kubla Khan":

In "Kubla Khan" if we yield, first, our senses, then our mind to its agency, we become conscious of the poet's interpretation of feelings so deep and so remote, though latent in phenomena, that we hardly suspected their presence, and hardly acknowledge them when represented. Yet, the more we train ourselves in this perception, the more joyful and wonderful life becomes, and the better we are able to appreciate the revelation of the poets of the nineteenth century.

This being so—it being the supreme office of poetry to

summon us to an unimaginable region of beauty, not to be expressed logically in words, though it may be suggested by the medium of words—it will follow that the whole structure of poetry will be super-rational, that the poet will use means for which no logical justification can be found. Mr. Magnus illustrates this text by the example of Tennyson, who, as a systematic and philosophic thinker, may be neglected, who as a poetic craftsman cannot be too highly esteemed. He shows how Tennyson chose his words as an Oriental goldsmith chooses his jewels, rejecting all but the most exquisite, fitting those that bear every minutest test into a perfect mosaic, in which every separate beauty bears its part in the beautiful whole. I recommend all who desire to excel in literature to study Mr. Magnus's analysis of Tennyson's method—to note how not merely every word, but every letter, has its significance. "Tears, idle tears" is one of the examples chosen, and, as the writer says, so wonderful is the making of this poem that "we notice—or, rather, we hardly notice—that there are actually no rhymes."

There are a few points in Mr. Magnus's book which seem to me arguable. The author thinks that the condition of the bourgeoisie of England—Dickens's great subject—has improved since Dickens's day. I doubt this. Mr. Micawber would not be sent to gaol in these days, but I do not think that he would have the spirit or the skill to brew a bowl of punch. Then I am not of the opinion that "Jane Eyre" is the most notable book written by the three Brontës. "Wuthering Heights" is, I believe, one of the most notable books in all literature: it is a Melchisedek of a book, without any traceable pedigree or derivation.

Edgar A Poe

POE THE ENCHANTER.
A Study in Æsthetics.

The name of Edgar Allan Poe was once mentioned in Emerson's presence. The sage of Concord lifted his eyebrows, and said, "Oh, the jingle-man!" and changed the subject. One understands the point of view; Emerson had read "The Bells" and perhaps "The Raven." Then there are many readers to whom Poe appeals as a capital concocter of "shockers"; others who rather like his detective stories; others who pronounce his work morbid and unnatural; and some who think he was a bad man given to excess in drink. I believe, indeed, that Poe's intemperate habits have excluded him from an edifice in America, called the Temple of Fame—a circumstance which must move the Shades to inextinguishable mirth. And it may be as well to say at once that all these criticisms are mentioned that they may be dismissed as impertinences and irrelevancies. Poe is one of the most important figures in the whole history of the fine art of letters, and those who have not been initiated into this mystery must be requested to regard themselves as profane, unfit to approach the shrine and oracle of the great American.

I am glad to find that Mr. Arthur Ransome,[1] author of "Edgar Allan Poe: A Critical Study" (Secker. 7s.6d. net), is fully possessed of the true faith as to Poe. He analyses the collected works of his author with that subtlety and sense of æsthetic beauty which they demand; he is absolutely convinced of the supreme dignity of the masterpieces on which he comments. And his study is "critical"; it is not a mass of undiscriminating laudation, of that "praise, praise, praise" which is the negation of the critical spirit. And I cannot help announcing my gratification in the discovery that Mr. Ransome feels about Poe, as I have always felt. I have always

---

1 Arthur Ransome (1884-1967) would become famous as a children's author and was later was suspected by British Intelligence of being a Soviet spy.

been convinced of the fact that Poe's work is supremely great, that the charm of it is unique in letters; but I should have been perplexed if I had been asked to justify this belief "in black and white," to give plain reasons for the faith that is in me. So Mr. Ransome:

> I had become dissatisfied with my own respect for Poe, because I could not point to tales or poems that accounted for its peculiar character of expectancy. I admired him, but, upon analysis, found that my admiration was always for something round the corner or over the hill.

Well, as Mr. Ransome says, very truly, "an admiration or contempt that we do not try to understand is more humiliating to the mind than none at all," and so he has written this study to justify to himself his sense of Poe's value. What is the secret? According to the author, Poe's supreme merit is not to be sought in the excellencies of his poems, or tales, or critical writings, but in the fact that he "tried to teach, even in broken speech, the secret of beautiful things, and the way not to their making only, but to their understanding." Poe's palmary greatness then, according to Mr. Ransome, is as a discoverer of æsthetic principles in literature, and I am not quite sure that I agree. Let it be understood that I quite admit the excellence of Poe's æsthetic work, considering the circumstances of the man's life and his surroundings, considering the nature of the barbarians amongst whose tents he dwelt, to whose deaf, and stubborn, and evil ears he preached his sublime doctrine, considering his reward poisoned arrows of calumny, and the sharp stones of starvation—considering all this achievement in proclaiming the first principles of art was little short of miraculous. He told that stiff necked generation that the object of poetry is to create beauty, and, consequently, to excite joy in that beauty. To us this is a commonplace; but to Poe's audience it was nonsense, and blasphemous, immoral nonsense, and just the sort of delirious wickedness that you might expect from a man who took more drink than was good for him. We can laugh at these people whose descendants are apparently in charge of the American Temple of Fame; but I agree with Mr. Ransome in thinking that the prophet who prophesied such things to such an audience is, indeed, an amazing figure.

Still, we must not forget Carlyle's very valuable caution—forgotten by Carlyle himself now and then—that the difficulty or ease with which a thing is accomplished has nothing really to do with the worth or worthlessness of that thing. A bad poem may have been written with great difficulty, and an immortal lyric may have flowed from the pen in an hour or two. Besides, I do not believe that Poe's vision of essential principles in art is the supreme reason for our admiration of his work. I am inclined to think that Mr. Ransome is nearest to the mark in that sentence, "My admiration was always for something round the corner or over the hill." "Over the hill"; exactly. Other writers show us the hill of our mortality—the side visible to us all; they picture to us the long white road thronged with the pilgrims of this earthly life; but in Poe there is the ever-recurring hint, expressed by mystic symbols unintelligible to the profane, that over the hill there are forms and figures of which we have never dreamed; that round the corner of that road there is an unimaginable country. Take for example the famous "Fall of the House of Usher." Considered from the point of view of the logical understanding, I could not justify my conviction that this is one of the finest stories that have ever been written. Logically, you have here a tale of an old house, of a melancholy brother, of a sister who is apparently dead, who rises from the death-chamber to affright the living, of the brother's madness, and of the house itself falling asunder and crashing down to destruction. Honestly, I cannot say that this plot, *quâ* plot, strikes me as a work of supreme genius. Indeed, I think I could name many better inventions by writers of quite inferior excellence. But read the story and meditate on it; contemplate the extraordinary atmosphere with which Poe has invested the tale; consider the mysterious thrill with which you are affected. You will find, I think, that you experience sensations and emotions similar to those produced by listening to wonderful music; you, have been charmed by a certain combination of sense and sound and suggestion, into another world; you have ascended the hill, and looked on a wizard land; you have seen the dread vision that lies beyond the corner of the road. Then there is another tale, called, I think, "A Story of the Ragged Mountains." It is, on the face of it, a tale of reincarnation; and, again, though the thing is deftly done, I cannot find the highest merit in the logical invention of it. But there are a few words descriptive of those forlorn and outland hills, of the mists and heats that brood over them, that sound on the ear like a spell, that echo within the spirit an unknown, unearthly message, from a world that is beyond the veil.

I have spoken of music and of charms and spells; and here, I believe, we must seek for the palmary excellence of Edgar Allan Poe. Allowing him, with Mr. Ransome, all his merits as a discoverer in æsthetics, giving him due praise for invention that is sometimes supremely good, for craftsmanship that is often superb in its accomplishment, I hold that his great secret lies in the fact that he was an enchanter, that he approximated to the primitive incantation, which is the essence and fount and origin of all true literature; that his work was of the family of "Kubla Khan." Pater,[2] whom Mr. Ransome calls an unconscious follower of Poe, laid down the far-reaching law that music represents the point to which literature should aspire; it is, another way of saying that literature should be an incantation. It should rise, that is, into a world which is above all logical definition, which cannot be explained in terms of the understanding or in terms of common sense, for the good reason that it transcends all these things; it speaks a language that is not of earth; in the last resort it is the communication to mortals of immortal and ineffable beauty. And all through the work of Poe, with varying degrees of intensity and clearness, we can hear the solemn and awful cadences of this in expressive song. As men in the market place, buying and selling, cheating or being cheated, speaking of common things in common tones, hear now and again the far-off triumph of the organ, and clear voices chanting the eternal mysteries, so in the tales and poems of Edgar Allan Poe there is a secret sense beneath the open sense, the sound of a voice that is not of man.

---

2 Walter Pater (1839-1894) was an influential literary critic and essayist.

G. K. C. ON G. B. S.[1]

I have always had a great admiration for Mr. G. K. Chesterton. To begin with, he is on the right side—that is to say, my side—and, secondly, those who are most perversely on the wrong side cannot deny that he has defended orthodoxy and attacked heterodoxy with wonderful wit and acumen and inventiveness. And therefore, because I admire Mr. Chesterton, I wish that he would not perpetrate such errors as this "Introduction to the First Edition" of his "Bernard Shaw" (Lane. 5s. net). Here it is:

> Most people either say that they agree with Bernard Shaw or that they do not understand him. I am the only person who understands him, and I do not agree with him.

Now, the second sentence in this "Introduction" is a flagrant specimen of the Impertinent Jest, more familiarly called the Silly Joke. And, furthermore, the passage in question belongs to a species of the genus, in question of which I, for one, am desperately tired. I find it difficult to pin the proper label on this particular kind of humour; but I suppose it may be called, for the moment, at any rate, the joke "per impossibile." It is based on the syllogism: "Nobody in his senses boasts of his superiority. I am in my senses, and I do boast of my superiority. Therefore it is very funny." I don't think that it is very funny. If Mr. Chesterton really believes that he alone understands the thought of Mr. George Bernard Shaw, then he is guilty of that "insolence" which, in Greek Drama, drives men to destruction. If he does not believe in his unique faculty of interpretation, then I think that he is not amusing, but merely stupid. Moreover, he is not original. In the course of his amusing, suggestive, and instructive criticism,

---

1 For Machen's coverage of Shaw's rebuttal to Chesterton, see page 133.

Mr. Chesterton draws attention to the very point that I have been labouring as a chief fault in his hero. Mr. Shaw will make silly jokes, says Mr. Chesterton, and I quite agree that many of Mr. Shaw's jokes are to me utterly stupid and wearisome. Mr. Chesterton gives some examples of this sorrowful defect. There is the stuff about Mr. Shaw being on Shakespeare's shoulders, which, if it means anything, means that Mr. Shaw is greater than Shakespeare, because he was born in the eighteen hundreds, whereas Shakespeare was born in the fifteen hundreds. Then Mr. Shaw says that Christmas Day is only a conspiracy kept up by poulterers and wine-merchants from strictly business motives; on which dictum Mr. Chesterton observes that it "is not so much false as startlingly and arrestingly foolish. He might as well say that "the two sexes were invented by jewellers who wanted to sell wedding-rings." Then, again, there is the joke in "Caesar and Cleopatra" of making the ancient Briton exactly like a modern Englishman. This, again, Mr. Chesterton reprobates, and still more the author's explanation that all characteristics are due to climate, and that "whatever races came into the English or Irish climate would become like the English or Irish." Then there is the "jest" that photography is more exquisite and imaginative than portrait-painting: all those follies are duly arraigned by the critic with sound and excellent sense. Mr. Chesterton, indeed, takes the pains to show that these and similar propositions are not true. I don't think that that matters a jot. There are plenty of lies which are capital fun. But these lies are so ineffably stupid.

I think that Mr. Chesterton is very sound on the main question of G. B. S. Mr. Shaw is a man of the most brilliant abilities and only two intellectual faults. He believes with all his heart and all his soul and all his strength in that which has no existence, and he scouts the existence of the only true realities. In other words, he is seriously of opinion that a settled income all round would make everybody happy; while on the other hand the true realities of man and man's life, such as poetry, romance, love, religion, are to him fictions and hallucinations, and mischievous hallucinations at that. Here, I think, we have the two primary falsities which underlie all his teaching. A fixed income is not the one thing needful to human happiness; poverty is not the one evil which makes happiness out of the question for any man. And a man utterly devoid of poetry, love, romance, and religion would not be a man at all. I do not know what he would be; I only know that I hope that I shall never meet such an one. It is true that the negation of all that makes life worth living is not wholly without experiment; there are hints of the attempt to realise the mechanical man in Dickens's "Hard Times"; there are more forcible hints still to the same effect in all our great industrial centres, those hints being written in dreary brick and stone and drearier lives. I do not think that it is necessary to labour the argument; it is enough to say that a man with plenty of food is by no means of necessity a happy man, and that any philosophy which proceeds on the assumption that such a man is necessarily happy is fundamentally and irrevocably false. Man's chief food is not bread; it is to be sought in all the regions which Mr. Bernard Shaw declares do not exist.

> When people asked Bernard Shaw to attend the Stratford Tercentenary, he wrote back with characteristic contempt: "I do not keep my own birthday, and I cannot see why I should keep Shakespeare's."

This instance of Mr. Chesterton's illustrates very well Mr. Shaw's nescience of all the things that are of any consequence.

George Bernard Shaw is, in fact, an instance of the most brilliant intellect exercised chiefly on false premises, and Mr. Chesterton shows, it seems to me, how such an antinomy became possible. Mr. Shaw was born, as his critic says, in an atmosphere which was Puritan and yet deliquescent. The Puritanism of the "English Pale" in Ireland has lost the old burning fervours, the great guiding principles of the seventeenth century. It has retained, unfortunately enough, all the irritating taboos of the Puritan system. Without the flame that burned in the Covenanting heart, it tries to keep "the Sabbath" after the

Covenanting fashion. It was this array of taboos that confronted G. B. S. under the great style and title of Religion; and G. B. S. decided, sensibly enough, that if Religion were such as this, then Religion was not for him. It is a pity, as Mr. Chesterton says, that Mr. Shaw did not discover that the religious principle has other representatives than Orangeism. Still, he did not do so, and here, I think, we find a clue to his dislike of some of the best things in the world.

I do not like Mr. Chesterton's manner of suggesting an antithesis between ethics and art. There is no such antithesis. Nothing can be beautiful (in the highest sense) and also immoral. Prettiness and immorality are quite compatible; beauty and immorality can never dwell, together. Still less do I like the reduction of this imaginary antithesis to concrete examples—to comparisons between Mr. Bernard Shaw—personating, apparently, the Good and the Ugly—and Messrs. Wilde and Whistler, who, I suppose, are the Beautiful and the Evil. We are judging the three artists by their works as creative artists, and I suppose there can be no doubt but that Whistler is by far the greatest of the three. If we are to judge them by their jokes, my personal vote goes to Mr. Oscar Wilde.

But, with all minor deductions, I think that Mr. Chesterton's book is to be highly recommended to all thoughtful readers. It is a remarkable study of a remarkable man; it abounds in controversial matter, in propositions with which many readers will be in violent disagreement. And, though I do not say that the quality of exciting violent disagreement is the one quality of good criticism, I do say that without this quality no really fine criticism can exist. The critic, if he be more than an entertaining chatterer, goes down to first principles, and first principles, on which so many of us differ, are the only principles which are really are worth debate.

WAS DICKENS A SOCIALIST?

It used to be remarked, I believe, that the sting of a lady's letter was usually to be found in the tail—that is to say, in the postscript. There may be a good deal to be said for this plan as a device of rhetoric, but I do not think I shall adopt it in noticing Mr. Edwin Pugh's "Charles Dickens: The Apostle of the People" (The "New Age" Press. 5s. net). Let me say at once, then, that I believe that Mr. Pugh[1] has written a book which was not worth writing; that he has employed his talents on a cause which is not worth defending.

Mr. Pugh's aim is this: first to prove that Dickens had the greatest sympathy with the sorrows and trials of the poor, and the greatest dislike of those persons who, by ill-will or incompetency or stupidity, embittered the lot of the poor. Well, the author has gained his suit, but then it was gained seventy years ago with the earliest pages of Dickens's work. And the second proposition is this: that Dickens was, in many ways, an unconscious Socialist, and that if he had been born a good many years later he would have been a professed Socialist. To which it may be replied that, on Mr. Pugh's own showing, Dickens was not in sympathy with technical Socialism, and that therefore there is no reason to suppose that dates would have made any difference to his beliefs. And behind all this there is, in my opinion, the last and fatal objection: that, literature is finally to be judged by literary canons, and that the social or religious opinions of men of letters are not of importance.

I know there is the other view, and I know that it is a very popular one. What were Emily Brontë's real beliefs? What convictions did Milton hold on the subjects of Sabbatarianism

---

1 Though Edwin William Pugh (1874-1930) was a prolific novelist, he is now largely forgotten.

and Polygamy? How far might Herrick be described as a Royalist? Was Shakespeare a Democrat? Was he an Agnostic—a Puritan—a Roman Catholic—an Anglican? These are all highly popular enquiries, and I think that they signify just as much as Homer's views on the Mediterranean slave trade—and that is not at all. Or rather—to qualify a little—shall we say, not very much?

And now, by way of proof of my proposition: that Dickens was in no sort or fashion an "unconscious Socialist," I should like to quote the author on the Brothers Cheeryble, who may almost be defined as Dickens's ideal of all that is good and gracious and lovable in man.

> But the Brothers Cheeryble are altogether abominable and raise our gorge. . . . [Dickens's description quoted.] This extract is given at length because it aptly expresses in its misguided love of its subject . . . Dickens's entirely false estimate of such people. There is a nauseous unction about all the descriptions of this old man and his brother and their ways that is nothing less than infuriating to any man who recognises what the existence of such characters really implies. . . . [the charity of the brothers described]. Thus he glorified the private charity of self-made plutocrats, which could be but the handing back, in paltry doles, of a portion of their unearned increment, the fruits of a wicked spoliation of the poor and needy.

Mr. Pugh further remarks that we have a Workmen's Compensation Act to meet such sad cases as that which Mr. Trimmers brought to the notice of the firm of Cheeryble—"smashed by a cask of sugar, and six poor children—oh dear, dear, dear!" Precisely; but Dickens did not think of the subject from the Act of Parliament point of view; he did not think of the brothers as bloated plutocrats and robbers of the poor. He thought of them as faithful stewards of the wealth that they had honestly—not oppressively or shamefully—acquired, as men who remembered the poor and needy in the time of their trouble.

Dickens may have been wrong, Mr. Pugh may be right; but it is evident from Mr. Pugh's own showing that Dickens was radically, fundamentally, and absolutely opposed to the first principles of Socialism.

And there is another point, quite unconnected with Socialism, to which I should like to draw my readers' attention. Mr. Pugh persists in treating Dickens's wonderful inventions, his unique fantasias on humanity, as if they were real people, as if one might meet them at tea. If this is to be allowed, farewell to our relish of Falstaff, farewell forever to Panurge and Brother John of the Funnels! But this is the way in which the author permits himself to write of Dick Swiveller and Mr. Micawber, those high immortals:

> He extracts an infinity of humorous enjoyment out of the miserable chicanery of such arch-wastrels as Dick Swiveller, where a man with a truer sense of equity in such matters would heap condemnation. His obliquity of moral vision in this particular arose, &c. . . . his childish recollection of the wretched Debtors' Prison . . . blinded him altogether to the consideration that the genteel person who lives by betraying the good faith of those who supply him with the necessaries of life is really a meaner sort of thief than the needy criminal.

Poor Dick! Whatever he may have been, he was not "genteel." And Mr. Micawber was worse, if anything. "An idle and self-indulgent rascal . . . who deserved a great deal worse than he got," selling his bedstead "in order to entertain his friends in riotous and wasteful fashion, whilst ruin brooded over his home and the hapless family dependent on him," and so forth, and so forth. Well, I suppose that Mrs. Micawber had no business to drink warm ale and to eat lamb chops, breaded. But, personally, I should not care to take counsel with a man who warned me against the morals of the gurgoyles on the cathedral parapet. Nobody wants to make a pet of a gurgoyle.

A GREAT EXPERIMENT.
Miss Evelyn Underhill's New Novel.

There is one thing, at all events, which may be confidently predicated concerning Miss Evelyn Underhill's new romance, "The Column of Dust'" (Methuen. 6s.).[1] It is one of the most daring experiments that have been made in literature. Kindly notice the precise phrase employed; I have not said that the book is one of the greatest ever written. But I reaffirm my description: it is a profoundly daring experiment. I do not know whether my readers are familiar with Miss Underhill's former novels, "The Grey World" and "The Lost Word." If not, I would advise them to make acquaintance with all three books at the earliest possible date. The trained and wearied reader of many novels knows to his cost the well-worn ruts in which so much of our English fiction rolls along. Miss Underhill has abandoned these ruts; she has found a secret path leading to an undiscovered country.

It is a salutary rule with most reviewers to exercise a certain discretion as to the plots of the novels which they criticise. The rule is a good one; but it would be difficult—or, rather, impossible—to say much about "The Column of Dust" without "giving away" the hinge on which the main interest turns. Here is the scene of the second chapter. It is in a book-shop, shuttered and barred for the night:

At 10 p.m. business hours were long over, and the place revenged itself upon intrusion by the uncanny air of peopled solitude, the suggestion that all trespassers will be prosecuted with circumstances of occult terror which lurks in empty houses, deep forests, and solitary shrines. Commerce was cast out, and seven other devils took her place.

---

1 Evelyn Underhill (1875-1941) was an Anglican mystic known mostly for *Mysticism* (1911) and *Worship* (1936). *The Column of Dust*, her third and final novel, was dedicated to Machen and his wife, Purefoy.

And in this empty shop stood the manageress of the business, Constance, the heroine of the story. She stood in a circle which she had traced on the floor, and the only light in the place was given by two candles of yellow wax, such as are used in masses for the dead. With much other singular apparatus, there was a brazier of burning char and on this charcoal Constance threw incense, and a thick white cloud arose. And then she began to speak:

> Ego Constantia conjuro te per Deum vivum, per Deum verum, per Deum sanctum et requantena.

"I, Constance, conjure thee by the Living God, by Very God, by the Holy God that reigneth for evermore." The fact was that this young woman, who believed in nothing in particular, who was perfectly healthy, and enjoyed the advantages of a University career, was attempting to raise a spirit by an ancient and picturesque process. She had no confidence that there were any such as spirits throughout all the wastes and immensities of the universe; she had less confidence in the queer formulæ of the mediæval "Grimoire," but—she thought she would like to try the experiment:

> The stream of strange and twisted syllables, the unearthly wailing songs, the rhythms which made no appeal to the ear of sense, rose and lifted her with them; then gathered the whole strength of her spirit for the supreme statement of exalted and illuminated will: "Messias Soter Emanuel Sabaoth Adonay, te adoro et invoco."

And then she saw "a tiny disturbance on the ground, close beyond the edge of the charcoal ring," and the dust on the floor stirring and gathering together. Perhaps it was blown by the draught under the door?

The little column of dust rose with a curious spiral motion, as if it were impelled from within. It hung in the air—a grey, faint, cobwebby thing. And then she heard the crying of a sad and frightened voice.

The materialistic young woman from Girton who recommended "Christmas Books" to her master's customers and was a very successful "buyer," had found out that the old recipe was only too efficacious. This, then, is the thesis of the book; the dwelling of an unembodied spirit in a human body as the fellow and guest of the human spirit; and the astonishment of that unearthly guest at all the spectacle of earth. And I think that such a scheme as this justifies my phrase, "a daring experiment," as applied to "The Column of Dust."

And what of the success of the experiment? Well; I do not think that it is in the highest degree successful. I go farther, and say that I do not believe that it is in the power of man to make such a theme into a success. We can hint at the unseen world, we can symbolise it, we can trace, as it were, the shadow of it thrown upon this solid earth of ours; we can see the image of it "per speculum in ænigmate"—through a glass, darkly; but—and this is a very great but—we cannot incarnate the unincarnate. Miss Underhill has done her very best; she has done, indeed, exquisitely; but being mortal, she has not succeeded in putting on immortality. One shudders to think of what an inferior hand might have made of such a theme as this; and the success that has been achieved is a very high testimony to the author's imagination and sense of literature. But for all that, I cannot conceive, cannot realise an Unembodied Entity as a spectator of Musical Comedy or as a guest at a London "At Home."

Here, by the way, Miss Underhill is enabled to get her "comic relief." She shows us an unequalled gallery of occult "rotters"—of people who gabble about alchemy, who gabble about Egyptology, who gabble about Symbolism, who gabble about all things in heaven and in earth of which they have no understanding. There is no touch of exaggeration; indeed, it would be difficult to exaggerate the follies and insincerities of popular occultism—and possibly those who move in such circles may be able to dot some i's and cross one or two t's. I must say, in conclusion, that one of the most beautiful things in the book is the wonderful and convincing episode of the Holy Vessel of the Graal.

TRYING THE SPIRITS.
Father Benson's New Novel.

There are several ways in which it is possible to approach spiritualism, or spiritism. Most of us, I fancy, not being spiritualists, are content to set down the whole matter as a compound of fraud and delusion. Spirit-hands, we say, are the hands of Sludge the medium, or else they are inflated gloves at the end of a long stick. The raps are produced by a clever trick, possibly by the medium's finger-joints, possibly by his knee-joints, possibly by his toe-joints. The writing on the locked slate is mere legerdemain, helped out by the conjurer's "patter"; the "materialised spirit-forms" are Mr. Medium or Mrs. Medium dressed up in all sorts of odd disguises, in muslin draperies, or priest's vestments or nun's robes. When strange tones are heard, it is ventriloquism, not a voice from the "other side." Perhaps some of us may go so far as to admit telepathy and the subliminal self as possible agencies in certain spiritualistic marvels; for the rest, we say that it is all theatrical and Maskelyne and Devant. Then there is the view of the spiritualists themselves—the belief that the genuine phenomena are the work of the spirits of the departed. And then there is the view taken by Father Benson[1] in his curious and fascinating novel, "The Necromancers" (Hutchinson. 6s.).

Father Benson's hypothesis is, it would appear, that there are in the universe forces—personalities—of hideous evil, whose delight is in the ruin of humanity—in body, soul, and spirit. These demons—to give them their just name—can be evoked, he thinks, by the spiritualistic process, in some instances at all events, and those who assist in the incantation are in the gravest

---

1 Robert Hugh Benson (1871-1914) was from an ecclesiastical and literary family. The youngest child of an Archbishop of Canterbury, Benson was ordained to the Anglican priesthood before converting to Rome. As a writer, he joined brothers A. C. and E. F. Benson in creating supernatural fiction.

peril. For the "unclean spirit" delights, as we have seen, to make its habitation amongst the sons of men, and if there be in the circle any of those persons called "sensitives," or "psychics"— to use the deplorable phraseology of the séance—the evil spirit will take possession of them, or at least endeavour to do so. The result may vary with the personality attacked; the devil may manifest as "nervous breakdown," or neurasthenia, or madness, or dipsomania, or general and total moral collapse. This is the hypothesis as to spiritualism which is skilfully and impressively worked out in "The Necromancers"; and, whether the theory of causation be right or wrong, I do not think that there can be any doubt as to the soundness of Father Benson's analysis of the effects. We may have our own opinions as to the nature of electricity, but we are all agreed that it is dangerous to play with dynamos and live wires.

I should think that the author has mingled a good deal in the circles which hover about the foolish and forbidden and dangerous thing called "occult science." Here is a portrait of a lady which seems life-like:

She was busy with various very beautiful little emblems—a scarab, a snake swallowing its tail, and so forth—all exquisitely made, and hung upon a slender chain of some green enamel-like material. Certainly she was true to type. As the full light fell upon her it became plain that this other-worldly soul did not disdain to use certain toilet requisites upon her face; and a curious Eastern odour exhaled from her dress.

Fortunately Maggie had a very deep sense of humour, and she hardly resented all this at all, nor even the tactful hints dropped from time to time ... to the effect that Christianity was, of course, played out, and that a Higher Light had dawned ... it appeared that the lady did not go to church, yet that, such was her broadmindedness, she did not at all object to do so. It was all one, it seemed, in the Deeper Unity. Nothing particular was true: but all was very suggestive and significant and symbolical of something else to which Mrs. Stapleton and a few friends had the key. Mrs. Baxter made more than one attempt to get back to more mundane subjects, but it was useless. When even the weather serves as a symbol, the plain man is done for. ... It seemed that the psychical atmosphere of most modern houses was of a yellow tint, but that this one emanated ... a brown-gold radiance which was very peculiar and exceptional.

The lady described had enjoyed the advantage of a quiet chat with Cardinal Newman a few weeks before her appearance at the country house. It is pleasing to understand that the Cardinal has become broad-minded on the "golden shore," though he has no objection to bestowing the orthodox benediction on those who desire it. Indeed, it is reported—though Father Benson does not mention this—that the Cardinal once announced his appearance to the séance by uttering the solemn word "Benedictine"!

It is with these elements, and with others, not foolish, but terrible, that the author has compounded his story. The medium Vincent is, I think, a wonderful figure. Vincent is no Sludge, no clever charlatan. He believes thoroughly in spiritualism, he acknowledges the risks that are incurred, he thinks that spiritual disaster must be faced by the spiritualist just as physical disaster has to be faced by the Alpine climber or the Arctic explorer—and he really possesses certain "occult" powers. Vincent is, in fact, a powerful ally of the besieging evil principle, but he does not know it; and when the Shining Form appears in the likeness of the dead Amy he is convinced that the girl's spirit has "materialised." So the hero of the tale falls into Vincent's hands, with the most awful peril—almost into destruction of body and soul. The scene of the final struggle of the lad's rescue, is admirably described. It is doubtful, I think, whether Father Benson's spiritualistic theory is the true one. It may be suggested that the Force evoked in the genuine séance is rather impersonal than personal, rather psychic than spiritual. But "The Necromancers" is most decidedly a book to read.

THE LIFE OF THE WORLD TO COME.

"On the night of the 1st of February [1762] many gentlemen eminent for their rank and character were, by the invitation of the Reverend Mr. Aldrich of Clerkenwell, assembled at his house, for the examination of the noises supposed to be made by a departed spirit, for the detection of some enormous crime. . . . It is, therefore, the opinion of the (whole) assembly that the child has some art of making or counterfeiting a particular noise, and that there is no agency of any higher cause." I make this extract—relating to the Cock Lane Ghost—from that ancient and respectable journal, the "Gentleman's Magazine" (via Boswell's "Life of Johnson"), because I am afraid that it throws considerable light upon the methods and the spirit of the late Professor Cesare Lombroso's "After Death—What?" translated into English by W. S. Kennedy (Illustrated. Unwin. 10s. net).

Professor Lombroso[1] was well known in this country. He was best known, perhaps, for his brilliant hypothesis that genius is a form of epilepsy; and of all the darts of the "scientific" enemy there is none more deadly than this, which makes men's noblest gift an allotropic form (to adopt the jargon) of a hideous and terrible disease. So far as I can gather, the late Professor was a convinced and fervent "spiritualist"; and the book before me is a presentation of the spiritualist case. And I must say that I began to read "After Death—What?" with a feeling of the most respectful interest and anticipation. There is a certain belief abroad in these days—I do not know whether I should call it a superstition or not—that what a scientific man says is of more credit than what a country parson says. I knew that Lombroso was a scientific man, because he identified imaginative genius with

---

1 Criminologist Cesare Lombroso (1835-1909) was yet another scientist of the time who became enamored with spiritualism. Lombroso is the author of *The Man of Genius* (1889), a controversial study which sought to link genius to madness.

lunacy and fits; and I was, therefore, pleased with the thought of this eminently scientific writer championing the cause of angels. And I must confess that the first chapter did not disappoint me. Professor Lombroso tells us of the extraordinary case of "C. S., the fourteen-year-old daughter of one of the most active and intelligent men in all Italy."

Here are some of the most remarkable features in the highly remarkable case of "C. S.":

> While she had lost the power of vision with her eyes, as a compensation she saw with the same degree of acuteness (7 in the scale of Jaeger) at the point of the nose and the left lobe of the ear. In this way she read a letter which had just come to me from the post-office, although I had blindfolded her eyes, and was able to distinguish the figures on a dynamo meter. Curious, also, was the new mimicry with which she reacted to the new stimuli brought to bear on what we will call improvised and transposed eyes. For instance, when I approached a finger to her ear or to her nose, or made as if I were going to touch it, or, better still, when I caused a ray of light to flash upon it from a distance with a lens, were it only for the merest fraction of a second, she was keenly sensitive to this and irritated by it. … Later the sense of smell became transferred to the back of the foot; and then, when any odour displeased her, she would thrust her legs to right and to left, at the same time writhing her whole body; when an odour pleased her she would remain motionless, smiling and breathing quickly. … She later predicted things that were to happen to her father and brother, and two years afterwards they were verified.

Now all this is intensely interesting; even more interesting is the case of "Dr. C., one of the most distinguished of our younger savants." The doctor frequently "announced to his mother the arrival of a letter, or a person whom he had not seen and whom he minutely described." But he did more:

On February 4, 1894, he predicted the burning of the Como Exposition (which actually took place on July 6) with such firm assurance as to induce members of his family, who had had other proofs of the accuracy of his prediction, to sell all the shares of the Milan Fire Insurance Company for the sum of 149,000 lire.

Now, I hope my readers appreciate the extraordinary importance of this instance. It is a case of true prophecy; it is not explainable by any theory of telepathy or thought-transference. The assassin of Percival might, conceivably, have transferred his intent to kill to the mind of Williams, the Cornishman; there are many histories of premonition which admit of a like explanation. No such theory will serve our turn here. The burning of the Exhibition was accidental and not premeditated; and at the time of the prophecy the Exhibition buildings "had not progressed very far." Therefore, there being no design to burn in any man's mind, no such design could have been transferred to "Dr. C.'s" mind; and, therefore, again, we have in this instance an undoubted case of prophecy, pure and simple.

And here, I am sorry to say, is where the story of the Cock Lane Ghost, quoted by me in my first paragraph, becomes applicable. I may say, by the way, that I hold that the case for prophecy has been fully made out by evidence apart from the history of "Dr. C." But I must say also that I cannot accept Professor Lombroso as a trustworthy witness on this or on any other point. For the Professor quotes, amongst other evidence, the Cock Lane Ghost "case, examined by Dr. Samuel Johnson, Bishop Percy, and other gentlemen," as an authentic instance of "spiritism and the apparition of phantasms"—and we know what the instance is worth. The "Ghost" was a detected imposture; and it seems to me that if the Professor is thus inaccurate where he may be tested, we have no guarantee that he is not equally inaccurate where we have no power of testing him. The book is full of the most astounding feats performed by Eusapia Palladino and by other mediums; there are elaborate and technical accounts of the scientific instruments employed to render cheating impossible. Now Eusapia may have done these amazing things, and the instruments may be infallible; but we, who were not present, who are unacquainted with the potencies and properties of a "Gaiffe electro-magnetic mechanism, suitable for use as an qualified electric cut-off," are not to pronounce either a favourable or an unfavourable verdict. But we are amply qualified to detect the author's citation of a notorious imposture as evidence in favour of the "spiritist" hypothesis. And, again, it has been laid down on high judicial authority that what the soldier says is not evidence; and here we have Lombroso quoting Brofferio, who quotes "Jacob, prestidigitator of the Robert Houdin Theatre in Paris," and Bellachini, who told Slade that they could not do the things that he did.

Far be it from me to say that this volume disproves the existence of spiritualistic phenomena; but I will say that it does not prove the existence of things. In the author we have a man who breaks down over a crucial instance, who quotes modern witnesses of more than dubious authority, who deals in vague hearsay, who informs us that A told B, who has whispered it to C, that X is Y; we have, that is, an essentially careless and inaccurate observer. Of what value, then, are the stories of "C. S." and "Dr. C."? Of what account are the long and elaborate histories of Eusapia's "levitations" and "apports" and dreams and predictions? In this dim and surmised region of the spirit of men the sternest accuracy, the most rigorous exactitude of statement are necessary in the first place, the second place, the third place; and frankly, to use a vulgar phrase, I would not hang a cat upon the evidence of Professor Cesare Lombroso. As for the great and terrible question "After Death—What?" the answer of the author would seem to be: After death we shall be at the mercy of fraudulent and vicious persons called mediums, for the purposes of table-turning, furniture-rapping, and general idiocy, the latter term including some of the most ridiculous sculpture and the most incompetent drawing that the world has seen in a long and weary experience.

DEE AND KELLEY.
A Chapter in the History of Imposture.

It is long, I think, since I have read a sadder book than this biography, by Charlotte Fell Smith,[1] of "John Dee," the famous "magician" of the Elizabethan age. (Constable. Illustrated. 10s. 6d. net.) It stands to me, I confess, as a symbol, as a concrete illustration of infinite waste and folly and delusion, of the certain and melancholy doom that awaits the men who adventure forth in that quest which is called "occult." It is true that Dee's fate was not the worst of all; he was evidently a sincerely religious man, with a firm faith in God, and consequently he did not sink into the deepest depths of Malebolge, he did not proceed by certain well-known stages from the condition of dupe to that of deceiver.

John Dee was a Londoner. He was born of Welsh parents in the year 1527, and in 1542 left Chelmsford Charity School for St. John's College; He became a brilliant scholar: he was selected as one of the original fellows of the newly-founded Trinity College; he frightened the undergraduates with his mechanical stage-effects for a performance of Aristophanes' "Eirene"; he went abroad and met all the most distinguished scholars and physicists of his day, and in 1550, a few days after his arrival in Paris, he was appointed a public lecturer on Euclid "mathematically, physically, and mystically considered." As a mathematician he was almost of necessity an astrologer, and it was Dee who determined, at the request of Robert Dudley, a fortunate day for Queen Elizabeth's coronation. Now, all this seems the beginning of a career of high and brilliant promise; for the time there was nothing at all amiss in the astrological practice. Nay; the late Dr. Garnett, of the British Museum, a man of immense learning, was a sincere believer in the main principles of astrology, and

---

1 Charlotte Fell Smith (1851-1937) was an English historian best remembered for this work, which is considered the first biographical study of Dee.

I do not know what right you and I (who have not made the experiment) have to say finally and dogmatically that there is nothing in it. And then there was another interest of Dee's which was, at least, harmless, or better than harmless. It was called then "natural magic," and, if it reminds us a little of the toy-shops, we must remember that from this "natural magic" arose all our modern mechanical appliances. So Dee describes accurately:

> A diving-chamber supplied with air. . . . The brazen head made by Albertus Magnus, which seemed to speak; a strange "self-moving," which he saw at St. Denis in 1551; images seen in the air by means of a perspective glass; Archimedes' sphere; the dove of Archytas; and the wheel of Vulcan, spoken of by Aristotle; and comes down to recent workmanship in Nuremberg, where an artificer let fly an insect of iron, that "buzzed about the guests at table, and then returned to his master's hand agayne as though it were weary."

In all this we have the serious pursuits and the learned by-play of a good scholar of the age. There was something of Bacon in Dee's nature, and Dee was, it seems certain, a better man than Bacon. And then this learned, devout, and ingenious man began to gaze into crystals, or rather to get other people to gaze for him. From this moment his diaries are little more than the receptacle of the lies told him by impostors, and chiefly by the arch-impostor Kelley, the "sludge" of the Elizabethan era.

Dee did not begin this pitiable descent under Kelley's guidance. His first medium was one Barnabas Saul, a licensed preacher. Saul, by the occult arts, gives news of buried treasure: "great chests of precious books" were buried somewhere near Oundle, in Northamptonshire. There were no precious books buried near Oundle, in Northamptonshire. Saul was next visited by a "spiritual creature" who gave directions for "skrying" in the crystal. Later Saul was tried on some charge at Westminster Hall, and, though acquitted, saw no more visions. But poor Dee had eaten of the accursed fruit, and before long Kelley was upon him, under the alias of Talbot. Kelley was born at Worcester, in 1555. He left Oxford under a cloud. He stood in the pillory at Lancaster, either as a forger or as a coiner, or both. He then got into trouble for digging up a newly-buried corpse, "for the purpose of questioning the dead or 'an evil spirit speaking through his organs.'" Then, having discovered the famous powder of projection, turning all things to gold, he seems to have been at a "loose end," and settled on the wretched Dee, at Mortlake. There the Archangel Michael ordered him to marry, and so Kelley married Joan Cooper, of Chipping Norton, whom he treated with consistent unkindness. Henceforth the history of Dee is the history of the ridiculous nonsense and verbiage imparted to him, by Kelley, the said nonsense and verbiage being alleged by Kelley to proceed from the angels and archangels and all the company of Heaven.

I have sought in vain through the numerous messages recorded in this curious book for anything significant or even impressive. There are one or two dubious cases of possible telepathy; against these we must set columns and battalia of empty and foolish words. Foolish, I say advisedly, considering the source to which these communications are ascribed. It is necessary to tell the beginner in arithmetic that two and two make four. The information is true, it has its place in the elementary book, it is fit and proper where it stands; but if a grown man were to inform his friends quite gravely that two and two make four, those friends would wonder; and if a learned man told us that he had received in a crystal a revelation from an angel that two and two make four, we should stare. I do not know what we should do if we were informed, on similar authority, that the true sum of two and two is five-and-a-half. Dee got messages of both kinds. Here is an example of the former sort:

> Bridle the flesh. Riotousness is the sleep of death and the slumber to destruction. Feed the soul, but bridle the flesh, for it is insolent. Look to your servants. Make them clean. ...

Persevere to the end. Many men begin, but few end. He that leaveth off is a damned soul.

This communication, said Kelley, came from the Archangel Gabriel. A little later the spirit Nalvage gave "an interesting geographical lesson about unknown parts of the earth," and Dee verified the lesson in the charts of Mercator and Pomponius Mela. Then Gabriel prescribed for Mrs. Dee, who was ill. She was to take "a pint of wheat, a live pheasant cock, eleven ounces of white amber, and an ounce of red wine, all distilled together." The moral lesson and the geography lesson seem superfluous; the prescription is fantastic to our ears, but would probably appear commonplace enough to the dispensers of the sixteenth century. But at last the spirit Madimi orders the Dee household to have everything in common, including their wives, and "poor Mrs. Dee ... fell a weeping and trembling," and then burst into a "fury of anger." Poor woman! And to crown all, "a little spirit, Ben," burst into a torrent of false prophecy, foretelling the death of Queen Elizabeth some sixteen years too soon. The unhappy Dee died in a desolate old age. It is a satisfaction to record that Kelley came to a bad and violent end, being murdered, in all probability by one of the princes whom he had cheated with golden lies. But if we are inclined to look down upon Rogue Kelley's victim, let us remember that it is only a few months since the spirits of Gladstone and Disraeli were giving oracles in the columns of a great daily paper.

A STUDY IN FEMINISM.

In one of Mr. Mallock's books—I think in "The Individualist"—there is a great discourse of corked wine.[1] It is of a metaphorical corking of allegorical drink that the Individualist makes his discourse to the Socialist; he says, in effect—I have not got the book by me—"What is the use of you and your friends clamouring for this, that, and the other; for material comforts, pleasures, luxuries? Look at us; we have got all these things, and don't you see that they give us no happiness, that we are, vitally and essentially, not a bit better off than you? Believe me, the wine that you are so anxious to taste is corked; its rare savours are become nauseous; it is of no use to any human being." And I could not help thinking of Mr. Mallock's corked wine when I was reading "Elisabeth Davenay," by Claire de Pratz (Mills and Boon. 6s.).[2]

Elisabeth, the heroine of Mlle. de Pratz's novel, was a masterful young woman from a very early age. This is what her father had to endure from her:

> "I'm twelve now, and I know what I want upon most subjects," she said. "I shall be a writer eventually, and I want to learn English and go to England. I've read that English girls are very free."
>
> Davenay looked at his daughter with a puzzled glance. . . .
>
> "But don't you want to get married when you are grown up, like other girls?" he asked.
>
> "No," said Elisabeth. "I despise men. . . . Later on I shall write books like Madame de Stael and George Sand. But

---

1 William Hurrell Malloch (1849-1923) was a conservative thinker and economist.

2 Claire de Pratz (1865-1943) was a French novelist. W. T. Stead (see note on page 58) admired *Elisabeth Davenay* and believed the book ought to be read by all women and young girls.

I must learn English now. . . . When may I go to England, please?"

Emile Davenay was indeed perplexed. This was the first time his daughter had ever condescended to speak to him, and she showed signs of becoming a woman with a will of her own—the thing he most detested in the world.

Well, I'll think about it," he said. . . .

"Don't hesitate about it too long, father. It is July now, and I should like to go to an English school next term, please."

M. Davenay was evidently a weak man. He did not follow the obvious treatment indicated for a little girl of twelve who issues orders to her father, despises men, and predicts for herself a place amongst the immortals. Consequently, Elisabeth went to England, passed examinations, and, returning to France, achieved "economic independence"—that is, became a teacher in a Government school—and helped to found a Woman's Daily Paper. It was called "La Révolte." While Elisabeth was on the staff of this journal she met a publicist named André Nortier, who began his career by publishing "two or three novels of anarchical tendencies, and had devoted himself entirely to the education of the people." Elisabeth and André fall in love with one another, but Elisabeth has misgivings from the first. "If I become André's wife," she says, "my incipient intellectuality would merge into his"; and, again, "Passion would be stronger than my newly-acquired consciousness of self, and would submerge my incipient brain-power." So, after a hard struggle, she abandons André to an old love of his, and goes to England to found an English version of "La Révolte"; and, for all I know Elisabeth may at this moment be one of the watchers and waylayers who hide in organs, are latent under platforms, ring loud and brassy bells, wield horse whips on the quivering flesh of stewards, throw stones through windows, chain themselves up in the most unexpected places, and generally embitter the existence of His Majesty's Ministers.

I think that Mr. Mallock's parable of the corked wine is of very obvious application to Mlle. de Pratz's delicate and skilful satire.

Elisabeth and her friends are devoted to the vote; the vote rouses them at early dawn, soothes their sleepless hours, and mingles with their dreams. To Elisabeth the suffrage is like some holy and magical bird in an Eastern tale; it is their Aladdin's Lamp which will build palaces in the wilderness; it is their Sangraal, which will bestow the joys of Paradise on those who achieve it. In the days when Jane Brown shall be able to affix a cross to the name of Ann Smith on a Parliamentary voting paper, then all hurts and doles shall be healed, and sorrow and sighing shall flee away. And all these visions are so infinitely pathetic when one realises that men have had the vote for centuries, that the vote is now, practically, within reach of almost every man who wants it; and that so far Utopia has shown no signs of appearing, and that sorrow and sighing absolutely refuse to flee away. Of course, men have been as foolish as women; in their day they have ascribed the same magical virtues and high transmuting efficacy to the vote—when they did not possess it. It was to be the powder of projection, "glistening and glorious as the sun," turning all it touched to gold. Well, the great experiment has been made, the operation of the wise has been performed—and the lead, alas! still remains, heavy and unchanged, in the crucible; or, rather, as that greatest of Liberals, Mr. Gladstone, thought, has been transmuted into something much worse than lead.

It is nearly eighty years since the first Reform Act; and Dr. Saleeby is talking of the House of Commons as "the lethal chamber of the soul"; and Mr. Masterman looks round England and sees that nothing is very good. The political wine is surely corked, and corked very badly; but to Elisabeth Davenay the French Chamber and English House of Commons are holy places, and a Deputy from the provinces is considered an important and majestic figure. Of course, the aspirations of the lady and her friends are not wholly in the region of politics; they have their word to say on moral questions. Hear Elisabeth on the law of marriage:

> "I do not think, if you wish to have any chance of success
> with your more advanced ideas, that you ought to wish to

abolish marriage at once, but must seek rather to ameliorate the institution. For instance, divorce might be made easier."

"Certainly," said Lafargue, "it ought to be made quite easy. To my mind, there is nothing more immoral than to force two people to live together who both cordially wish not to do so. Divorce ought to be granted immediately upon mutual consent."

"Madame Danarr's League has long advocated that divorce should be granted after a direct appeal made three times by two married people before the Justice of Peace," put in Rudo. "That seems sensible. A man and a woman agree to disagree. They wish to part company, and therefore are entitled to formulate three appeals at intervals of three months each for the first two appeals, and of six months for the last appeal. Once the Judge has done all in his power to reconcile them and has not succeeded, then they ought to be set free by law. The children, if there are any, should be given in charge to the more worthy partner, or divided between the two. The Judge would decide that point."

"For my part," broke in Maria Lafargue, "I do not see why a woman should not be as free as a man to do as she will, and change partners as often as she may care to do so."

Well, this happy, holy vision has almost been realised in some of the United States of America, and to quote once more from Mr. Masterman's "Condition of England,"[3] the state of things in American Society is not exactly Edenic; it is described as "a nightmare and a delirium." The book, as a whole, is written carefully. Here and there one feels that the writer is thinking in French, not in English. There are two or three peccant "and who's," and I note the phrase "in fact and in deed," which seems pleonastic. I do not like "his fingers, like some tender octopus, found hers." But, as I have said, "Elisabeth Davenay" is a wonderful satire on the pathetic fallacies of the feminists.

---

3 Charles Masterman (1873-1924) was a British Liberal politician. Machen's review of Masterman's book appeared in the June 6, 1909 issue of *T. P.'s Weekly*.

THE GENIUS OF PERSIA.

Some months ago I read a very silly book. It was on education, and the author held forth on the absurdity of examining English students in Greek and Hindoo students in English. Now, I am by no means a "hard-shell" partisan of the Universities, but it seems to me that the course of action alluded to is eminently and entirely sensible. It is quite right that Indians should have to study Shakespeare; it is quite right that Englishmen should be obliged to construe Sophocles. It is right because one of the many uses of true education is to develop what one may call man's "intellectual body," to call into play intellectual muscles that, in the natural course of things, would become atrophied. And there is no better way of training these "muscles" than that of introducing the student to a world of thought strange, and alien, and unknown. If a man does nothing but walk, he only exercises certain parts of his body in a certain way; swimming adds to his stock, and rowing develops yet another set of forces and capacities. So, far from joining in the cry against "compulsory Greek," I should like to invent the very different aspiration of "compulsory Persian." And, if this were ever granted all else should be left in the hands of Professor Browne.

It is now many years since I read Professor Browne's[1] enchanting and wonderful book, "A Year Amongst the Persians." This was one of the few books which remain in the memory of the reader; devoid of the inanities, the stupid funniments, and tiresome and empty detail of so many works of travel, it gave me not so much the description of Persia as the sensation of Persia. Always, thinking of it, one smells the scent of the rose garden, always one hears the mystic song:

---

1 Edward Granville Browne (1862-1926) was an Orientalist scholar and Professor of Arabic at Cambridge who focused upon Persian culture, history and religion.

> The Kingdom of It we forsake,
> And your home in annihilation make[2]

always there is the dream of Narshisch, the colour of the wine of Shiraz, the ecstasies and martyrdoms of the Bâbis. And now from this most accomplished pen we have "A Literary History of Persia" (Reprint. Unwin. 12s. 6d. net).

As Professor Browne remarks, our earliest association with the word "Persian" is a Biblical phrase expressive of the unchangeable character of the nation, and it is a curious comment on the "that altereth not" that a modern Persian, if suddenly placed in the Persia of hundreds of years ago, would find but little difficulty in understanding and being understood. The nation has been conquered and reconquered again and again throughout the centuries, but its genius, its language survive; and, as the author of this "history" points out, the Bâbism of sixty years ago is but a reincarnation of certain theological and philosophical ideas which antedate the Mohammedan conquest. Nay, when Arabic became for a time the fashionable language of literature, the strange idiom was entirely permeated by the native genius, and so a great part of Arabic literature is in reality the Persian voice speaking through an Arab mask. The national spirit, however, survived the conquest of the horrible Mongol Hulagu, and in due season we may even see it surviving "Constitutional Government" and making poetry out of "Mr. Speaker," "Cheers," "Hear, hear," and "Laughter."

In this, the first, volume of his history, the author shows us the origins and dim beginnings of the people and the language. Here is an extract from an inscription of Darius at Persepolis:

> Saith Darius the King: When Ahuramazda saw this earth... then did he entrust it to me, He made me King, I

---

2 Previously, Machen had made use of this Sufi-infused verse for a short story entitled *The Rose Garden*, which was first published in *The Neolith* (1908), and later included in *Ornaments in Jade* (1924). No doubt, Browne's work inspired Machen's poetic tale.

am King, by the grace of Ahuramazda have I set it in right order, what I commanded them that was carried out, as was my will. If thou thinkest, "How many were the lands which King Darius ruled?" then behold this picture: they bear my Throne, thereby thou may'st know them. Then shalt thou know that the spears of the men of Persia reach afar; then shalt thou know that the Persian waged war far from Persia.

Apropos of later inscriptions of the same period, Professor Browne suggests a very curious subject of enquiry. The Macedonian conquest was near at hand, and the language anticipates, as it were, the temporary decay of the race. The grammar is decadent, deliquescent; cases and declensions are confused; and the author speculates as to whether this degeneracy of speech may be regarded as an omen of degeneracy of race. It would be interesting to apply this theory to modern languages; to speculate on the possibility of "sloppy" constructions and barbarous phrases being the outward signs of "sloppiness" and barbarism eating into the heart of a people.

One of the most important questions as to early Persian literature is, it seems, almost an insoluble one. Who was "Zoroaster"? When did he live? At what period were the sacred books of the "Fire-worshippers" written? What was their original language? These, says our author, are problems which admit of no certain answer. Geldner and Darmesteter represent the two extremes of opinion.

> According to the former part of the Avesta at least . . . represented the actual utterances of Zoroaster or his immediate disciples; Bactria was the scene of his activity, and its language the vehicle of his teaching; the King Vishtasp" . . . "has no place in any historical chronology" . . . . and the period at which he flourished may have been anything from B.C. 1000 to B.C. 1400.

Then, on the other hand, Darmesteter places the construction of the Avesta as late as the first century of the present era, and will allow the Zoroastrian creed a no more remote period of origin than the sixth or seventh century B.C. The question is not one for a layman's intervention; and here it may be proper to remark that, in a sense, Persia as always been a kind of Oriental America—in this one respect, that it has been from early times a hot-bed of strange and fantastic religious sects. Zoroastrianism had its heresies, and it is odd to think that Manes (or Mani), born A.D. 215-216, was the founder of a system which spread all over the West, which captured St. Augustine in his youth, which reappeared later as Paulicianism, and finally manifested itself in Provence as Albigensianism, and set Europe by the ears. Professor Browne does not note the fact, but I believe that Manicheism lingered on amongst the mountains of South-Eastern Europe as late as 1750, and it is possible that its spirit, in a new guise, is one amongst the most important forces of our modern life.

I cannot help quoting a passage which gives the ideals of the pagan Arabs, before the coming of Mahomet:

> "Honour and revenge," in short, as Muir well says, were the keynotes of the pagan Arab's ideal "muruwwa" ("manliness" or "virtue"); to be free, brave, generous; to return good for good and evil for evil with liberal measure; to hold equally dear wine, women, and war; to love life and not fear death; to be independent, self-reliant, boastful, and predatory; above all, to stand by one's kinsmen, right or wrong, and to hold the blood-tie above all other obligations, such were the ideals of the old pagan Arabs.

I think that this is a remarkable passage, since it seems to me that there is a nation still in existence whose religion, whose idea of "virtus," is remarkably akin to that held in pre-Mahommedan Arabia. Many of Professor Browne's most interesting pages deal with the curious interplay in theology, politics, and literature of the rough, downright Arab, with the delicate and mystical Persian; and, so far as I can gather, the author is of opinion that while Arabia was the strong arm of the new religion, Persia was certainly its brain.

I must end this article—which does not pretend to be a review, but merely to be an indication of one or two points out of many—by quoting some beautiful lines by the Sufi poet Jami:

Thou art Absolute Being; all else is naught but a Phantasm.
For in Thy universe all things are one.
Thy world-captivating Beauty, to display its perfections,
Appears in thousands of mirrors, but it is one.
Although Thy Beauty accompanies all the beautiful,
In truth the Unique and Incomparable Heart-enslaver is one.[3]

---

3 Jami (1414-1492) was an influential Sufi mystic and poet. This poem is found in Browne's book, *A Literary History of Persia* (1902), which Machen had probably read.

THE HOLY SEPULCHRE.
The Pope's Desire to Have it Brought to Rome.

A few days ago the morning paper contained a singular paragraph. Ghalib Pasha, who accompanied the Ottoman mission to Rome on the accession of the present Sultan, was conversing with His Holiness respecting the establishment of a Nunciature—a Papal embassy—at Constantinople, and while this official point was being debated the Pope asked the Turkish diplomatist whether the Sublime Porte would consider the question of selling the Holy Sepulchre, with a view to its being transferred from Jerusalem to Rome. Ghalib Pasha, it is reported, said that he had no authority to treat on this subject; but it is added that the Holy Father intends to persevere and seek the good offices of the German Emperor, with a view to securing for Rome the holiest of all Christian relics. And it is curious to think that a somewhat analogous proposal, coming from a different quarter, brought about the Crimean War of fifty-odd years ago.

The Holy Sepulchre is a true Holy of Holies. It is the inmost and most sacred shrine of the Church of the Holy Sepulchre, which is, as it were, a nest of hallowed places and chapels and memories and objects—a pageantry of the mysteries of the Christian Faith. Here are to be found the tombs of Adam, Melchizedek, Joseph, and Nicodemus, forerunners and attendants of the Cross; here, too, are the graves of Godfrey and Baldwin, the great warriors of the Cross in the Middle Ages. Here the faithful are shown the sacred places of the Passion and Resurrection; here are the chapels of the Blessed Virgin Mary, of the Mocking of Christ, of St. Helena, of the Penitent Thief, of the Invention (or Finding) of the Cross. And all the rites of Christendom have here their recognition and their several altars: Latins, Greeks, Copts, Armenians, Maronites, Syrians are represented, and I believe that of late years the Anglican Liturgy has been celebrated at one of the altars of the Eastern obedience. And the heart of all this is the Chapel of the Holy Sepulchre. You enter the antechamber through a low door, and see a representation of the stone that was rolled away from the door of the Tomb; and then, within, is the true Chapel of the Sepulchre—a cell six and a half feet long, six feet wide, and very low. And here is the hollow in the rock—the new tomb which St. Joseph of Arimathæa placed at the service of the disciples of the Lord. Before the Sepulchre forty-three lamps burn continually. Such is the Great Relic which the Pope wishes to add to the holy possessions of the Roman See.

Before we trace the history of the Places, it must be said, by way of explanation, that the early Christian Church was profoundly sacramental in its feeling, in its teaching, and in its practice. That is to say, it was always seeking for an inward and spiritual grace beneath an outward and visible sign. Differing from the Gnostics—whom certain very foolish persons of our days pretend were the only real Christians—the Church held that the material was good, as the immaterial was good; that the material owed its virtue to the fact that it was both the manifestation of the spiritual and the veil that covered and sometimes the outward thing was the very channel by which the inward grace was conveyed. Thus, the sick, we are told in the Acts of the Apostles were healed by handkerchiefs which St. Paul had touched. By a natural consequence, the outward sign was regarded with a certain reverence: thus the Christians, from the earliest times preserved with veneration the relics of the martyrs—as in the case of St. Polycarp, the disciple of St. John the Divine. And thus, from the first ages, the Christians went on pilgrimage to places hallowed by their associations, and above all to the scenes of the Passion and Resurrection of Christ. We have no authentic history of the Holy Places for the first few centuries; tradition says that they were defiled by heathen temples being built on them. A chapel of Jupiter, they say, occupied the place of Resurrection, and an altar of Venus that of Crucifixion. But, when persecution ceased, Constantine the Great directed that a splendid church should be erected over the sacred sites, and this church was consecrated in the year 335.

Of course, the whole question of the site has been disputed; but, waiving the intricacies of this debate, which is rather for experts than laymen, there is certainly no à priori impossibility or improbability even in the existence of certain place-traditions for three hundred years. There was a Fairy Rath in Ireland which had always been held to be a fortress of the "little people"—flames had been seen to issue from the summit of it. And a hill was excavated, few years ago the and it was found that the "little people"—the primitive Turanians—had really lived there, and that flames had no doubt issued once on a time from a choked-up shaft which led from the place of the fire. But that "once on a time" must have been nine hundred years ago! However that may be, from the time of Constantine the tradition of history. the Holy Places becomes history. The church was the central point for the devotion of the whole Christian world; it was at Jerusalem that a lady named Thuria saw the bishop using incense towards the close of the fourth century. The first shock came at the beginning of the seventh century, when the Church of the Holy Sepulchre was desecrated by the Persians, who carried off the True Cross and took the Patriarch of Jerusalem prisoner. In 635 it is said that the succeeding patriarch, Modestus, recovered the Cross and restored the church. But later in the same century came the Saracens, who captured the city and the church, restoring the latter to the Christians, in the hope of propitiating Charlemagne. On his death the infidels again took possession, and finally the Turks became the masters of the Holy Places, and, it would seem, only refrained from levelling all to the dust on account of the tribute which they exacted from the unceasing stream of pilgrims. But they were not content with tribute; the pilgrims were subject to insult and outrage, to every kind of danger and ill-treatment. Robert, Duke of Normandy, father of William the Conqueror, who made the pilgrimage in 1035, describes his journey to Jerusalem as a journey to Paradise under the conduct of devils; and no doubt, if a great feudal prince suffered considerable discomfort at the hands of the Mahometans, a poor man would suffer very much worse things. And so came Peter the Hermit, the Knights Hospitallers, the Templars, and the Crusaders. One can read in history—and in "The Talisman"—of the great exploits and adventures of Christian and Paynim Knights, of how whole armies of crusaders perished on the way for want of direction, how others went marauding over the lands and cities of their fellow-Christians of the East, and how, after a possession of about eighty years, the Cross fell before the Crescent in 1187. It is possible that the loss of the Holy Places accounts, in part at least, for the sadness with which most of the great Legends of the Graal (which were being written in those days) close the story of another Relic. The Crusades, indeed, continued, but without any useful result, and the last of them was led by our Edward I. in 1270. Ever since the year 1187 the Holy Sepulchre has been in the possession of the Turks. Still, the pilgrim ages have never ceased, and the Pope's desire to add the Sepulchre to the local treasures of the Roman Church is evidence that the old devotion is as great as ever.

And the brief moral is that all this history that I have compressed into such a dry and desiccated condition—all these singular actions, from the fervent devotion of the earliest pilgrims who travelled through wild and evil lands in wild and evil days to see the holy place, from the great church built by the Roman Emperor, from the growth of Templarism, from the long wars of the Crusades, even to yesterday's ambition of the Roman Pontiff all these things were done and endured and desired from the merest sentiment. It may be said—I am quite sure that it has been said—that true Christianity is an inward and spiritual life, consisting in the holding of a certain faith, in performance the of certain actions, and in the abstinence from certain other actions—not in travelling a long way to look at places which may be wrongly located, or to kiss objects which may possibly be forgeries; that in any case the money and energies expended, on pilgrimage would be better bestowed in the service of the poor. Be that as it may, it cannot be denied that the devotion to the Holy Places is a sentimental devotion. And I would merely ask my readers to imagine—if they can—a world wholly devoid of sentiment.

A NEW YEAR MEDITATION.

I want to enter into competition with Mr. Sherlock Holmes—or rather, perhaps, with M. Dupin, the great detective of Poe's imagination. We all know, of course, that if we placed before either of these personages a little tooth-powder, a bunch of violets, and the *Hypnerotomachia Poliphili* we should immediately arrive at the most astounding and unexpected results; and so I hope to deduce odd conclusions from three recent events, all chronicled in the daily paper. In the first place, Mr. H. G. Wells has published his novel "The War in the Air," wherein we are instructed that the whole fabric of civilisation is destined to utter destruction and ruin. Secondly, the yearly address delivered at the meeting of the Egypt Exploration Fund showed that in prehistoric times the Egyptians kept pet dogs, whose bodies have been found braceleted about the legs with ivory, whose teeth show traces of over feeding and systematic pampering. Thirdly, the records of the Birmingham Police Court have dealt quite lately with the adventures of five boys charged with breaking into a number of houses at Harborne. "Their abode," said the police, "was a cave which they had constructed at Florida, a lonely district near Harborne Golf Links. Investigations showed the cave to be partly a natural declivity and partly an ingeniously-constructed hut, formed of interlaced boughs. Grass and soil laid on the top formed a perfectly rain-proof roof. This was supported by stout balks of timber. The walls and floor of the hut had been carefully lined with straw."

Now, I submit that these three items of news, incongruous as they may seem, have, in spite of all appearances, a certain relation to one another. To take Mr. Wells's book in the first place. I do not know, nor do I suppose that Mr. Wells knows, the precise manner and fashion in which the present structure of things which we call Modern Civilisation will be reduced to dust and ashes; but we may be sure that somehow or other the fabric of our social order will sooner or later come thundering to the ground: commerce, and manufactures, machines and great cities, economic systems, means of communication—all these things are destined to pass away as the old empires with their civilisation have passed away. The world will go into the melting-pot again, and the Roman Empire will be repeated in a very different form. But in a certain way the results will be similar. A highly-artificial state of things will be succeeded by a barbarous and natural state of things. Perhaps a man who wants a knife will not be able to buy one in Oxford Street or in Bond Street, for the reason that both streets will be heaps of ruins overgrown by trees and flowers. The man in need of a knife will be obliged to make it himself as best he can; and it is likely enough that the man incapable of making knives (or spears or swords) will find himself hopelessly handicapped, and doomed to perish. In a word, the arts and crafts will be born again in a world where dilettantism has, perforce, ceased to exist; in a world of sincerities. There will be painting in this new world, as in the old; but nobody will be inspired to paint pictures of fox-terriers capering about a little girl and a Persian kitten. Poetry will be rude enough, but it will be the expression of sheer ecstasy, not to be repressed or controlled; people will dance, but they will not waltz; there will be strange songs, but no musical comedies.

It may be said that it is impossible to prophesy; but I think that this opinion is mistaken. I think that the instance of those prehistoric pets of prehistoric Egyptians—one instance out of many possible instances—shows that humanity, in spite of surface changes for good or bad, is radically immutable. There is, I know, a sort of assumption, usually rather implied than expressed as a definite proposition, that modern man is really a different creature from mediæval man or ancient man or prehistoric man; that a cabbage has somehow or other turned into a rose-tree—or, if you like, that a rose-tree has become a mangel wurzel. For the last hundred years or more one has encountered this "transformation-scene" hypothesis or assumption; some people will date the beginning of the miracle from the fall of Constantinople, others from the Reformation, others from the French Revolution. And yet—to take the last date of transmutation—I have met peasants who don't care twopence for M. le curé, and spend considerable sums with "le grand divin" when their cattle are out of sorts. And I suppose that "palmists" and astrologers gain a very pretty living from the pockets of well-educated people in the London of to-day. Then there is another region: one has heard that the reign of brute force is over. But if that is the case it seems a pity to waste such a lot of money on "Dreadnoughts" and "Invincibles" and "Collingwoods." No, it seems to me that humanity is always humanity. It may be bound down by all kinds of conventions; it may be caged up by every sort of rule and regulation; but it remains unaltered, both for good and for evil. The lion of the Zoo is essentially the lion of the desert. This may be demonstrated by the simple and pleasing experiment of throwing open the gates of his cage.

Probably the boys who recently appeared before the Birmingham magistrates were the children of comparatively well-to-do parents; they were burglars and cave-dwellers not from necessity, but from choice. The boys "bolted" to the best of their ability from civilisation; they made their own house instead of the houses that had been made for them; they won their own food by their own wit: they returned, in a word, so far as they were able, to the primitive state. A most interesting example. It shows that the secret has been kept; that in spite of the yearly, monthly, hourly work of the enormous machine that we call civilisation the human spirit yet remains, unchanged and unchangeable, ready, when the opportunity occurs, to wipe out all the lines that have been ruled for it, and to write again the ancient hieroglyphics in place of the modern commercial hand. No doubt those Birmingham boys will get into sad trouble, since so long as the present social structure endures our larders must be protected; and yet in their doings I find grounds for a great optimism. For the whole note of our modern civilisation is that everybody is engaged in "dry nursing" everybody else, and the dry nursing is all done by machinery. Now, the fact is that man's happiness really depends on the exercise of his creative faculties, of the power given him of making all sorts of things with his own brains and his own hands; and some have hoped and many have feared that those faculties were becoming more and more atrophied, so that in a hundred years or so nine-tenths of the human race would be unable to do anything beyond touching an electric button. And if this were really the truth, we can see that the inevitable collapse of modern civilisation would lead to the extinction of a hopeless and a helpless race.

The secret, as I say, has been well kept through centuries of mechanical oppression; in the heart of man there is still the desire of making, of inventing, of creating. At first in the new age the faculty will be utilitarian; the spear to kill the game and the pot to cook it in will be the things needful. But the spear will be a real spear made out of the man's own head; it will not be a feeble, second-hand copy of some spear made three thousand years ago. And the maker of pots will have no South Kensington Museum to go to, so that he may imitate, very badly, pots that cooked Trojan dinners during the great siege. And from this compulsory sincerity, and from the desire of the beautiful and the wonderful that is part of man's unalterable nature will rise the new art, the new literature, and the new music.

The Blue Saucer of Bristol

Some time ago a friend of mine was telling me of a curious adventure that had befallen him at Bristol. The scene was the "artists' room" of a concert hall, and my friend, who was waiting there, was suddenly startled by strains of very indifferent violin music. "Why on earth are they playing that stuff?" said he. "Oh, don't you know," replied the lady to whom he had spoken, "the Cup has commanded it!"

I believe my friend was somewhat mystified, and I am sure my readers will be mystified too. And I hope they will not be too irreverent when I inform them that "the Cup" which bespoke the dubious melody is said to be the very Holy Grail of the mediæval romances! Well, in the first place, it is not a cup, it is a saucer of bluish glass, and its history is roughly as follows. Twenty years ago, more or less, Mr. A. was in the Riviera, and had his attention called to a curious vessel for sale in a local shop. For reasons unknown to me he bought the blue saucer that was shown him and took it home. His father immediately said that he must have it, "as it was most important." When Mr. A. succeeded to his father's estate, he promptly took the vessel and buried it in a well at Glastonbury again for reasons unknown to me. Then, after certain years, the Misses B. began to see visions and dream dreams; and the result was that the blue saucer was found by them at Glastonbury and taken to Bristol, where, after certain vicissitudes, it still abides, reverenced as the vessel in which Christ "made His Sacrament," as the old romances have it. I give for what they are worth the following "occult rumours": "At present it is in a private oratory, and people with psychic gifts see rays of light issuing from it, or an angel guarding it, or, again a star above the house. A wonderful spiritual influence is said to pervade the place, and those who go there in distress of mind come away comforted." I give also for what it is worth the rumour that the late Sir John Evans, the famous antiquary, pronounced the vessel to be a forgery of modern date.

But the curious point is this. Mr. A., the original "discoverer," evidently imagined that he was restoring to Glastonbury a holy relic which pertained to that famous abbey. Now, considering what Glastonbury was actually claiming in the twelfth century, it may seem odd that it did not claim the possession of the Holy Grail; but, as a matter of fact, it did not do so. The body of King Arthur was "discovered" at the abbey; the miraculous altar of St. David, called "the Sapphire," was also in the possession of the abbot; and William of Malmesbury hints that somewhere or other in the precincts lay buried St. Joseph of Arimathea and with him two vials containing the Precious Blood. But nothing is said about the Holy Grail; perhaps for the good reason that in the year 1130 or thereabouts the myths of the Grail had not yet taken shape. I am afraid, therefore, that I have not the smallest belief in the Blue Saucer of Bristol; but I should like to recommend to my readers Mr. T. Scott Holmes's "Wells and Glastonbury," which Messrs. Methuen are publishing. For, apart from myths old or new, Glastonbury is a place of perennial interest. It was probably one of the earliest inhabited places in Britain—there was a lake dwelling close at hand—it was, very likely, one of the earliest seats of Celtic Christianity; its name, Ynys Wytrin, the Glassy Isle, attests its sanctity in Celtic eyes, and, so far as I know, it was the only English monastery which had a continuous existence, without a break, from Celtic to Saxon times. And I wish I knew how it became identified with Avalon, the Apple Garth, otherwise the Celtic Paradise.

And here is another question: I have just said that "glassy" meant "holy," "mystic," "magic," to the Celts. This was so; but why was it so? In one legend Merlin vanishes in a "glassy boat," and St. Columba received a "glassy book" from the hands of an angel.[1]

---

1 For more on Machen's scholarly approach to the Grail legends, see *The Sangraal* essays in *The Great Return* (Darkly Bright Press, 2017, pp. 65-98).

How to Enjoy Life

The Lowly Man who Masters the Art of Being Ignored

Arthur Machen
From a Snapshot

How to enjoy life? There is no easier question than this. The answer is to be found in Thomas à Kempis: Ama nescriri, et pro nihilo reputari. (Love to be unknown, and to be held of no consequence.)

And as Joubert says: "The philosopher, the good man and the saint are all happy, but the saint is the happiest man of all, so much is man made for sanctity." The matter is simple, then: if you wish to enjoy life, embrace the career of sanctity.

But—there is no denying it—there are people who, for one reason or another, seem incapable of the career in question. They have no vocation for it. But still the great maxim of à Kempis applies.

A few years ago, when my habitation was among the tents of Fleet Street, I thought to give a brother journalist something of a shock by quoting to him the "Love to be unknown" dictum. I thought he would be amazed, almost dumbfounded, to hear of this world of the cloister, so utterly remote from the world in which we moved, of a life which avoided all the goods of the life of the streets, and indeed held our blessings for its curses.

Never did an attempted surprise fail so lamentably.

"I know," he replied in his calmest tone. "Thats what old Billy Wembley always used to say. He was a bit before your time, I think; but everybody in the Street knew him. I've often heard him say: 'I don't want them to know I'm there, old chap.' He used to send in a couple of 'sticks' to one paper, the same quantity to another, a stick-and-ball to a third, and perhaps a solid half-column to a fourth; all regular stuff. And as he used to say: 'You see, I'm nobody; I don't take much space, and I don't draw much money from any one of them; and so, when they're spring-cleaning, they get rid of the people who write special articles and sign them and want a lot of money. They leave me alone; they say old Billy's stuff is always all right, and doesn't cost much anyhow. And that's the way I generally make eight or nine quid a week. *They don't know I'm there.*'"

I don't suppose that the late Mr. Wembley had ever heard of Thomas à Kempis, and I am quite sure that he would not have been interested in the ghostly book if he had seen it; but he applied the saint's maxim perfectly. He enjoyed life because he had mastered the art of being ignored and held of no consequence. He that is down need fear no fall, as Bunyan puts it.

But, then, again: you may not possess this lower vocation of undistinguished respectability. You may be a wastrel, a ne'er-do-well, a good-for-nothing, with extremely low tastes. Still, the great maxim holds. When Little Dorrit was born in the Marshalsea Prison, the medical man in attendance was a certain Dr. Haggage, himself a prisoner. Mr. Dorrit was glad to hear that his lady was "doing charmingly."

"Though," he added, "I little thought once that—"

"That child would be born to you in a place like this?" said the doctor. "Bah, bah, sir; we don't get badgered here; there's no knocker here, sir, to be hammered at by creditors and bring a man's heart into his mouth. Nobody comes here to ask if a man's at home, and to say he'll stand on the door-mat till he is. Nobody writes threatening letters about money to this place. It's freedom, sir; it's freedom! I've had to-day's practice at home and abroad, on a march and aboard ship, and I'll tell you this: I don't know what I've ever pursued it under such quiet circumstances as here this day. Elsewhere, people are restless, worried, hurried about, anxious respecting another. Nothing of the kind here, sir. We have done with all that—we know the worst of it; we have got to the bottom, we can't fall, and what have we found? Peace. That's the word for it. Peace."

And then, as Dickens relates, the happy doctor went back to his associate and chum in hoarseness, puffiness, red-facedness, All Fours, tobacco, dirt, and brandy.

And so, when you ask the secret of enjoying life, you get the same reply from the Catholic saint Thomas à Kempis; from the Protestant saint Bunyan; from the steady professional man; from the wastrel and runagate. Whatever ladder you are on: get to the bottom of it and stay there; it is the only station which is happy and secure. And I remember another witness to the truth of this great paradox. In Zola's "L'Œuvre," the old painter, of established fame and honour, is talking to the young men with all their work still to be done. "Ah," said he, "you young men will never believe it, but I can tell you that happiness is to be found at the bottom of the mountain, not at the top. I am at the top, and I am the wretchedest of men."

It is a tremendous paradox; if one assents to it, the words will stick in one's throat; it goes utterly against the grain of humanity; but I believe it to be true. Of course, there must always be a certain reservation: one thing required. St. Thomas à Kempis did not want to be looked up to in his monastery; but he wanted God. The industrious journalist did not want to be pointed at as that brilliant fellow Wembley, "author that wonderful series of articles on Bimetallism that everybody is talking"; but he wanted to be certain of to-morrow's dinner. Dr. Haggage did not want to be a famous Corinthian and the chief friend of the Prince; but he wanted brandy.

The violent paradox resolves itself as we look at it into the merest common sense. Be quite sure what it is that you want; and see that you get it. But if you would do that, you must disregard all the non-essentials, the mere trifles and trappings of your career. And these prove in the long run to consist of what other people say of you. Dante Gabriel Rossetti, I am sure, desired to write well. But he desired also to be praised for writing well; he wished to be known, and so, when a book of his was to be published, he plotted, and contrived, and conspired so that the new volume should fall into the hands of the "right" reviewers.

He was miserable man. At last he allowed Buchanan's silly "fleshly school" attack to drive him crazy. But St. Thomas à Kempis and Dr. Haggage knew each what he wanted and wanted alone; and each obtained his desire and enjoyed peace.

Part Three

Selections from
The Literary Week

THE LITERARY WEEK.

September 18, 1908

This I will say, that anyone who has really taken one of the great undoubted masterpieces to his heart, who has read and re-read it, so that it has become a familiar inhabitant of his mind, will never admire rubbish. He may be lightly amused by rubbish for an afternoon—there are times when purposeless nonsense is better than a fortnight at the sea—but he will never call a trashy, vulgar, pretentious writer "great." I defy anyone who really knows his "Don Quixote" ever to decline seriously upon twaddle, ever to give to pompous trash the same kind of love or praise that he has given to the best romance in the world.

...

Amongst the minor classics I should like to place a book which I have just been re-reading—for the twentieth time, I suppose. It is but Mrs. Gaskell's "Life of Charlotte Brontë." Where Lockhart failed Mrs. Gaskell triumphed. But her "Life" is a work of art; it is a composed and perfect picture of Charlotte Brontë, and of the terrible and tragic environment in which she lived. You can hear the wind "wuthering" round that grim parsonage amidst the graves, on the height of those dismal rolling moors; you feel the tragedy of those lives, the horror that surrounded them as the mists surround the bleak hills. Lockhart, on the whole, has kept the curtain down; Mrs. Gaskell has raised it. And I read only a week or two ago a letter in a paper from a gentleman who is quite certain that Charlotte Brontë, not Emily, wrote "Wuthering Heights"! It was to confute the statement that Currer and Acton Bell made their famous journey to London, and disclosed their true identity to Mr. Smith, the publisher. This was 1848; let us meditate on the persistence of error. The odd thing is, that such a blunder was ever made. A not very scrupulous publisher was its inventor, but one cannot understand a sober critic believing for a moment in the identity of "Currer" with "Ellis." "Jane Eyre" is a remarkable book indeed, but "Wuthering Heights" is a work of the highest genius.

September 25, 1908

And here is another matter for congratulation. Mr. Henry James's novels and tales are to be published in a collected edition by Messrs. Macmillan. Many years ago a brilliant essayist said that Mr. James wrote as if writing were a painful duty. There is truth in the criticism, but it is not all the truth. Personally, I like Mr. James's best work in spite of his manner, rather than because of it; but his best is certainly very good indeed. He did some admirable work for the "Yellow Book"—one remembers the "Death of the Lion" and the "Coxon Fund." The latter tale was, I should think, suggested by the life of Coleridge; the former seems to refer to a great man who is still with us. Mr. James is at his happiest in dealing with personalities of men of letters. But his "Turn of the Screw" is one of the very best horror stories ever written.

October 9, 1908

I am curious to know whether Mr. Algernon Blackwood (the author) and Mr. Eveleigh Nash (the publisher) will find their account in the poster advertisement of "John Silence." I remember that Mr. Le Gallienne's "Quest of the Golden Girl" was advertised very effectively in this way, and the late Guy Boothby's "Dr. Nikola" was at one time on every boarding. I have not read "John Silence," but if it is anything like "The Listener," by the same writer, it must be very good indeed. I should place that story of the men on the island amongst the whispering, mysterious voices of the willow lushes in the very first rank of tales of terror.

...

I wish somebody would write a little tract on the "Psychology of the Howler." I don't mean the schoolboy's howler or the undergraduate's howler—these are the bright children of Ignorance and Imagination. The howler that interests me is the error which flows from the pen of the well-informed writer in a moment of aberration—or possession by some envious fiend. I once translated a French book, and the fiend in question whispered in my ear that a certain passage required a footnote. That was a lie to start with; a note was absolutely unnecessary. But what followed was worse. I may not know much Latin; but I do know that "quasimodo" does not signify "a little while." Yet I explained it in that sense in my note. It has been on my mind for twenty years, and I have kept it dark to the present moment, though "The Scarlet Letter," "The Silence of Dean Maitland," and "Michael and His Lost Angel" are all favourites of mine. But the consciousness of sin softens the heart, so I can feel for the weekly literary paper which informed its readers a few days ago that Anne Brontë wrote "Wuthering Heights" and that Jeremy Taylor did not belong to the seventeenth century.

October 16, 1908

I wonder whether my readers are familiar with an odd masterpiece by Mark Twain called "Life on the Mississippi." I hope they are for their own sakes, as it is one of the most delightful and wonderful of books. Those who have not read of the Admirable Bixby, who have no knowledge of the manner in which that "Lightning Pilot" brought his boat through the shoal water of the Hat Island crossing, should run at once to Messrs. Chatto and Windus and buy the illustrated edition. But my point is this: here is a most enchanting book, more richly stuffed with adventurous matter than ninety-nine adventure stories out of a hundred; and yet its subject matter is the intensely technical art of navigating the Mississippi River. The moral is that there is nothing more delightful than technique if it be well-handled, and the stranger, the more remote the technique, the better we like it. I think this is one of the reasons why people like to read about the players; they want to go "behind the scenes," to read of the strange and elaborate mechanism by which scenic effects are produced. So Miss Terry's reminiscences are delighting us all; so one book about Irving succeeds to another.

...

Miss Braddon has just celebrated her seventy-first birthday, and I am sure that we are all glad to congratulate her, and to express our thanks for her honest and excellent achievement—excellent in its way; for though a "Braddon novel" is not a piece of curious literary art, it is always an example of sound craftsmanship, without pretence, without false ornament or meaningless flourishes. I suppose that the school which Miss Braddon founded, the school of fiction which may be classed under the heading of "Domestic Sensationalism," is derived, in part at least, from "Jane Eyre." There is usually a mystery and often a murder; but the problem set in the first chapter is generally solved by the play of circumstance, and not by the conscious intervention of a Dupin or a Sherlock Holmes. And, by the way, I wish Miss Braddon would tell us how she came to write "Ishmael." It is not, I think, one of her great successes, but it shows a most curious and intimate knowledge of the manners and customs of the Parisian workmen. Again the interest of technique! It pleases me to read that the old cabinet-maker had *pieds de mouton à la Ste. Menehould* for dinner, more especially as Miss Braddon tells us exactly how much his dinner cost him.

October 30, 1908

Mr. H. M. Schroeter, of Los Angeles, announces for 1909 "A Bibliography of the Rubáiyát of Omar Khayyám, with Notes for an Anthology of Kindred Literature." Any notes and suggestions will be welcomed by the compiler. I have no doubt the book will be an excellent one, but I cannot help being reminded of the lines:

> There was an old person of Ham,
> Who got tired of Omar Khayyám.
> "Fitzgerald," said he,
> "Is as right as can be,
> But that 'Club' and those 'Versions' oh, d-n!"

It is clear, of course, that the old person had never been invited to the Omar Khayyám Club.

...

In Mr. Bernard Capes's new novel, "The Green Parrot," the hero flies from the world because he finds that there is no appreciation of the "style" which he puts into his books. And I wish someone would inform the readers of T.P.'s WEEKLY what "style" really is. The true "stylist" is never difficult, though his subject matter may be obscure; indeed, the more subtle and mystic the thought, the more lucid becomes the expression of it. Rossetti used to read old books in order to find "stunning" words to put into poetry; we may doubt whether this is the true path to the great manner, and when we read Christina Rossetti's best work our doubt will, I think, become a certainty. "All affectation is bad," said Don Quixote to the boy of the Puppet Show; and it is to be surmised that the writers who have achieved style never set themselves deliberately to become "stylists." I think that if Stevenson had lived he would have recognised that the "sedulous age" must be shaken off. And as for a definition of style, perhaps it would be as vain to demand a definition of the wonder of the dawn.

November 13, 1908

Mr. W. Ayott Orton's essay on "Walter Pater" in the November "Westminster" lays the stress on the pagan form of the great author's thought. It is but fair to remember, however, that "Marius the Epicurean" shows a profound sympathy with certain aspects of Christianity. The description of the Eucharist of the early Christians for instance, has appeared, and on just grounds, in a volume of selections from the Christian Mystics. Mr. Orton shows that there were moments in which the external world appeared to Pater as something hard and unsympathetic; unknown and unknowable. But Marius saw, as he says, the things of the external world receive meaning and beauty and purpose in the Christian offering; and perhaps in the last resort Pater, like Marius, was an *anima naturaliter Christiana.*

...

It is almost cowardly of the "Simplified Spelling" people to put Professor Skeat in the vanguard of their battle. They are aware that all the world reverences Professor Skeat's profound philological knowledge—the Professor now and then writes in the "Academy" the history of a word, and makes it better reading than a fairy tale—and they know that the unsimplified spellers will not dare to jeer. Nevertheless, I am with Mr. Chesterton; "holiday" shall never be "hollidi"; and the simplified shall stretch their racks and heat their pincers before "through" shall be "thru." No doubt Professor Skeat is right in saying that our spelling often obscures the real history of a word. It obscures the history of the word; but it illuminates the history of English learning, so that a superfluous letter is a hieroglyph of the Renaissance.

December 18, 1908

Reputation is never safe. M. Edmund Harancourt, the French poet, lecturing the other day at the Grafton Galleries, told his hearers that La Fontaine was an Anarchist, "because he had no respect whatever for the family, the law, or any of the fundamental principles of society." Quite so; and where will you find more revolutionary treatises than "Alice in Wonderland" and "The Hunting of the Snark"? The latter work, no doubt, shows the impossibility of attaining Absolute Truth. It is the text-book of a monstrous skepticism.

...

That reminds me of Mr. Wells, who, I see, says that logic is a broken reed. Well, if Mr. Wells denies by precept, many writers show their contempt for logic in the most forcible manner possible—that is; by practical neglect. I noticed curious evidence of this when reading Mr. Chesterton's "Orthodoxy." Mr. Chesterton is attacking Mr. Suthers, who said (I think in "New Age") that freewill was lunacy because it meant causeless actions, and the actions of a lunatic are causeless. Now, this syllogism is precisely as if one should say: Men are birds, because men have two legs and birds have two legs. But Mr. Chesterton, instead of pointing out the "Undistributed Middle," contents himself with "denying the major"—i.e., he says that the actions of lunatics are not causeless.

January 8, 1909

Apropos of "glas" meaning "woad" or "blue" in Welsh, it is interesting to note that the Welsh word and our "glass" are first cousins. We will still think of "bright red" and "bright blue" in ordinary conversation; and it would seem that our remote ancestors were apt to look upon colours as different forms of brightness—as I suppose they are, from a scientific point of view. So Cæsar translates "glas" into "vitrum," which means glass; so "glaucus," the Latin equivalent of "glas," meant originally gleaming, while "glaux," the Greek for an owl, is as much as to say the "glaring" bird. And the root of "purpureus," purple, which was applied to things so different as a scarlet robe and a white swan, signified in the first place to gleam or shine.

...

I hope that none of my readers is indulging in sorrowful meditation on the effects of "the festive season." If there be any such, let him bear his pain like a man for the sake of old customs. For England was always renowned, not only for the quality, but quantity of its Christmas cheer. It is amusing to note that Brillat-Savarin boasts that the word "gourmand" is untranslatable. The author of the "Physiologie de Goût" does not admit, I think, the term "gourmet." In France I was taught the following three degrees: The gourmet signifies a man who likes a little food, exquisitely prepared; the gourmand is for quality and quantity too; while the goulu is our English glutton.

February 12, 1909

According to Mr. Andrew Lang, Mr. Van Gennep, a French authority on Homer, is absolutely orthodox. He will have nothing to say to those who "split the 'Iliad' and the 'Odyssey' up into hundreds of shivered potsherds, of all sorts of distant ages, by innumerable makers." The "Higher Criticism" will some day adorn a curious chapter in literary history. I remember that many years ago the "Guardian" treated one of the "Higher Critics" on his own principles. I believe he turned out to be at least three gentlemen at once.

...

It seems that, according to Mr. Bernard Shaw, America is to be saved from the eternal fires at Doomsday by the intercession of Poe and Whitman. I think that the name of Hawthorne should be added. "The Scarlet Letter" is certainly one of the finest romances that the world has produced.

February 19, 1909

It is to be hoped that Mr. Oliver Madox Hueffer, the expert on witchcraft has had his attention called to a recent correspondence relating to the Anti-Vivisection Society. A member of the society, a lady, has been threatening prominent vivisectors with "death by prayer," and the secretary, Mr. Stephen Coleridge, has written to the papers—firstly, disclaiming any official connection with the lady's threats; secondly, acknowledging the effects of "malevolent suggestion"; and, thirdly, appealing to all anti-vivisectors to make "precatory efforts in my defence, in order that I may not fall under the malign influence created by the force of malevolent suggestion which may possibly be exercised against me by the vivisectors, and by Lord Cromer's earnest associates in the Research Defence Society." And then there is still a more interesting point of view, suggested by another humanitarian enthusiast. Miss Woodward, the secretary of the Society for United Prayer for the Prevention of Cruelty to Animals, thinks that it may be as well to leave the vivisectors alone:

> *An unrepentant vivisector dead might do more harm to the community that a living vivisector. We can control the actions of the living, but we do not know what evil influences may be set at work by the uncontrolled spirits of the dead. It is at least a curious fact that our work was never so severely attacked as shortly after the death of several well-known vivisectors.*

I hope the purport of these quotations will not be misunderstood by any of my readers. I am not concerned either to attack the practice of vivisection or to defend it; I merely wish to point out that the doctrine involved in the expressions cited is purely and simply the doctrine of witchcraft—that one human being can slay another by the exercise of will-power. And Miss Woodward's theory of the malignant ghost is, perhaps, older even than the theory of witchcraft.

February 26, 1909

The were-wolf, in varying forms, is, I think, a mythos of world-wide extent. Mr. Harold Blind, writing in the "Pall Mall Gazette" on "Myths of the Monjik," says that the belief is still flourishing in Russia, and has been the cause of horrible violence committed on innocent persons. But were these persons wholly "innocent"? I am not hinting belief in the literal truth of the myth; but though human beings do not assume the form of wolves, there is no doubt that certain individuals in primitive races are subject to a horrible seizure, during which they suppose themselves to be wild beasts—and act up to the assumed character.

March 12, 1909

The other day I met a man of letters with a genuine admiration of the typewriter! I think the fact deserves to be recorded, since, to the best of my belief, the case is rare. For the most part the literary man—as distinct from the manufacturer of "marketable stuff"—likes to see the sentence grow under his hand in his own peculiar and characteristic script. I will not say that traces of the old love of calligraphy still linger among us, since we mostly scrawl. Still, a man's handwriting is in a sense a part of himself and an index of himself; and it is singular that an imaginative man should suffer gladly the typewriting "m." I do not know whether this weakness be not preferable to the great and universal weakness of "seeing oneself in print"—a desire which, coldly considered, appears in the highest degree paradoxical.

...

Tennyson thought that if we could understand the flower on the wall we would understand the universe. This we shall never do; but we can gain, a certain dim vision of the final mysteries through the eyes of childhood, and it is this vision that Mr. Algernon Blackwood has recorded in "Jumbo" (Macmillan)—a most successful essay on the most difficult of themes. If we could recollect certain of the thoughts of our childhood, we should all be men of genius.

April 2, 1909

The Feast of St. Patrick, which formed the subject of an article in a recent issue of T. P.'s WEEKLY, is celebrated after divers manners, and I am wondering whether any of my readers were present at Mr. Plunket Greene's beautiful recital at the Æolian Hall. If so, I hope that their curiosity was roused by the "Irish Idyll in Six Miniatures" by Miss Moira O'Neill, with music by Sir C. V. Stanford. For those who listened with delight to these exquisite poems, set with rare felicity, may desire to know more of Miss O'Neill's work, and so may purchase the complete volume, "Songs of the Glens of Antrim" (Blackwood). They will not be disappointed. There is a certain class of Celtic poetry which is often extremely beautiful, but which suffers, now and then, from its allusiveness, from its appeal to readers learned in all the strange and storied byways of ancient Irish mythology. At first sight the mere Saxon can make but little of "The Valley of the Black Pig." Doubtless the beast is highly significant, but he is puzzling to a stranger in the same manner as the Welsh "Hen-wen, the Sow of Dallwyr Dallben" is puzzling. Now, Miss O'Neill's poems have all the charm and mystery and sadness of the Celtic mind without the technicalities of some Celtic bards. Here, for example, are two stanzas of "The Fairy Lough":

Loughareema! Loughareema!
  Lies so high among the heather;
A little lough, a dark lough,
  The wather's black and deep;
Ould herons go a-fishin' there,
  An' sea-gulls all together
Float roun' the one green island
  On the fairy lough asleep.

Loughareema! Loughareema!
  Stars come out, an' stars are hidin';

The wather whispers on the stones,
    The flittherin' moths are free.
One'st before the morning light.
    The Horsemen will come ridin'
Roun' an' roun' the fairy lough
    An' no one there to see.

There is a rare and subtle music in these lines, as it seems to me, and
  "The Songs of the Glens of Antrim" is full of such work as this.

. . .

The following sonnet is submitted by a corespondent (H. M. W.,
London) to the judgment of the readers of T. P.'s WEEKLY. Mr.
H. M. W. says that he found it written, without date or signature,
on the fly-leaf of an old book, bought by him from a book-
barrow.

Whenas I pass in retrospect the last
Four years, those blissful years, by Fate's decree
Indelibly engraved upon my soul,
It seems a breath from Heaven so fleeting fast,
Enwraps my soul in pure sublimity,
And dips into Lethe's stream all thoughts of woe;
Within this time, my love was kindled slow,
Yet steadfast, as the flame at Vesta's shrine.
Her love is pure, yet doth each day as sorrow
Unto that all too heavy load of mine,
Each day has less sadness than the morrow,
Each moon doth less my soul with joy beshine.
My humble Muse herself bethinks, and saith:
"Must Love and Beauty not submit to Death?"

    Personally I am not inclined to attribute any great antiquity to
the above production.

April 9, 1909

A was talking to B the other day on the subject of communication
from the other world, and a letter, supposed to have come from

the late Mr. Myers, was read out. B sighed wearily, and said: "I thought we should have finished with the split infinitive on the Golden Shore."

...

In all probability few of the admirers of Francis Thompson's poetry are so much aware of the existence of a curious little treatise by him called "Health and Holiness" (Burns and Oates). There are some very significant things in the course of the essay; its main purpose is to show that the penances and austerities that may have been well-suited to the full-blooded men of the Middle Ages are perhaps hardly the best medicine for a modern citizen penanced already by dyspepsia, neurasthenia, and the rush of industrial life. There is a good story, too, in the book: A bishop is reported as saying that it is useless to put off the old man—in order to put on the old woman.

April 30, 1909

"Musical Telepathy: apropos of the 'Electra' of Strauss" is the title of a pamphlet published at Milan. The author gives a list of "hundreds of ideas" which, he says, have been "lifted" by Strauss from an Italian opera called "Cassandra" produced in 1905. As to all this, I say with Sancho: "I come from my vineyard; I know nothing"; but I like the title of the pamphlet. Telepathy is prettier than "plagiarism" and I am reminded that I have heard a similar charge conveyed under the style of "thematic coincidences."

May 7, 1909

"Genius is akin both to madness and inspiration." This quotation from a very remarkable article on "Genius" in the "New Quarterly" for April by the late Samuel Butler. But I wonder whether genius is akin to madness. I should have said that genius and madness sometimes have certain symptoms in common. A man of genius sometimes, but not always by any means ,exhibits a certain distraction of manner; and most madmen are, I suppose, distracted or liable to distraction. But, in spite of ancient authority, I doubt whether the resemblance is more than surface-deep. The madman looks wildly because cosmos in him has given place to chaos, because the central authority which rules the human polity is dethroned, bound in darkness. The madman looks wildly at the world because the world looks wildly on him; the order of the universe has become disorder and nonsense. But the man of genius, though his actions may sometimes resemble those of a madmen, is in a very different state. His distinction arises from the fact that his eyes are grown dim with gazing on too bright a splendour; he stumbles over a pebble because he has been viewing the glory of the sun. In the one case there is the confusion of excessive darkness, in the other the confusion of excessive light.

May 14, 1909

The centenary number of the "Quarterly Review" impels one almost inevitably to talk about Keats and to utter respectable commonplaces on the subject of criticism. The old theory that Keats was "killed" by Croker's stupid and offensive article is, I believe no longer held by any responsible person, though perhaps Croker—with the assistance of Maginn—may have discouraged the poet, and thus have deprived us of masterpieces. This in itself is a grievous matter enough, and I do not think that it is a defence of these literary criminals to say that they wrote in the fashion of their time. Insolence, malignity, offensive personalities are disgraceful in any age, near or remote, and I do not mean by this sentence to imply that true criticism should consist in the mere ladling out of laudatory "pap." It is sometimes the painful duty of a judge to order a man to be hanged by the neck until dead; it is sometimes the painful duty of a critic to tell an author that his English is faulty, his arguments fallacious, and his imagination a minus quantity. But it is never the duty of a judge to mingle with the dreadful utterances of doom sarcastic remarks about the prisoner's inferior social status; nor is it ever the duty of a critic to mention an author's connection with "gallipots," or to sneer at his poverty, or to insist on the fact that his work was originally printed in a journal purchasable for the sum of one half-penny. In the first place, such remarks are unmannerly, and therefore un-Christian, and secondly they are both imbecile and "impertinent"—in the technical sense of the word. A man quite badly off, who has never been visited by "the country," may write a masterpiece; and it is as foolish to talk about "halfpenny journalism" as it would be to speak of "Paradise Lost" as "Milton's five-pound epic," or to sneer at FitzGerald's quatrains because they found their way to the Penny Box.

May 21, 1909

Mr. Fagan, the author of "The Earth," has not been successful in his attempt to avoid the naming of an actual paper. The "Observer" has pointed out that there is a paper called the "Earth"; it is the organ of the people who are quite sure that the earth is flat. These "heretics" always interest me; I think it must be splendid to believe that Bacon either wrote or inspired the whole literature of his age, and that the Holy Graal is at present moment safely enshrined in Bristol.

…

"Creation and Criticism" is the title of a very interesting paper by Mr. C. L. Moore, reprinted in the "Author" from the "Chicago Dial." The writer might well have called his article, "The Paradox of Creation." He says, no doubt with truth, that:

> *the part which the naïve, the unconscious, the untrained faculties of man play in the production of literature was over-insisted upon in the criticism of the last century. It was held that the literature was the spontaneous speech of man … the great existing epics of the world were divided into two classes, the naïve and the artificial.*

Mr. Moore, questioning this view, points out that there is as much art in the "Iliad" as in "Paradise Lost": that no literature, however early, can exist without method, artifice, conscious work. But he might have gone further and demonstrated that the finer the masterpiece the more elaborate the form. The hexameters of Homer are not a disorderly and unmarshalled rush of words; and the white fire of Sappho is run into a strict and cunningly proportioned mould. The discovery that Beauty is to be found in shapeless disorder is wholly modern.

128

The Literary Week

June 4, 1909

I am afraid that the judicial must admit that Mr. Andrew Lang was right in the advice which he gave the other day on the subject of authorship. Mr. Lang was speaking at the annual dinner of the Royal Literary Fund, and

> *His advice to the ardent youth who thought of commencing as an author in the field of history, poetry, the essay, literary criticism archæology, anthropology, and so forth, was "Don't." These were not studies which supported the student.*

Mr. Lang went on to apportion the blame for this state of things. Partly, as he said, the authors are at fault, because they write dull books; but the chief sinners are the reading—or, rather, the non-reading—public. The people who spend money like water on motor-cars and bridge, and such-like diversions, grudge ten shillings for a book. True; but the reason of this economy is plain enough. The man who pays a thousand pounds for his motor-car does so partly out of ostentation; but chiefly because he likes motoring; he abstains from the practice of book-buying partly because a good library has ceased to be a necessary piece of state for a rich man, but chiefly because he does not liking reading; or, to carry the matter a stage further, because he does not like thinking. There, I suppose, we must stop; the next cause would have to be expressed in Sancho Panza's formula: "We are all as God made us, and most of us a great deal worse." So, thinking being generally a somewhat unpopular diversion, the author will be, as a rule, a poor man.

. . .

There are, of course, exceptions to the general rule. Now and than an abstruse book becomes popular and a source of income. Take, for instance, "The Rosicrucians: Their Rites and Mysteries," by the late Hargrave Jennings. I am afraid that his work is nothing more or less than an undigested farrago of curious nonsense; yet it has been reprinted again and again. I suppose the glamour of the word "Rosicrucian" has had something to do with the popularity which the book enjoyed and enjoys; and the author's attitude as of one who tells a little, but could, if he would, tell a great deal more, was, no doubt, found to be attractive.

July 2, 1909

A creed called "Futurism" is expounded by M. Marinetti in the review "Poesia." It was M. Marinetti who declared, according to the "Evening Standard," that "a race-automobile adorned with great pipes like serpents with explosive breath, a race-automobile which seems to rush over exploding powder, is more beautiful than the victory of Samothrace," and the application of this dogma is to lie in the destruction of all museums and all libraries. This is a new reading of the old saying, "Destruction to those who said all good things before our day!" It would certainly be a great comfort, if one were writing an epic, to know that there was nothing to be feared in the way of comparison or competition from Homer, Virgil, or Milton. There is something very insolent about the past.

...

Apropos of the recent production of "Louise," a weekly a paper says that England is not "a Symbolical nation." I hope that this pronouncement is mistaken, since all fine art is essentially and necessarily symbolical. Art is the presentation of images with symbolism ideas or emotions. A Turner picture is not the mere likeness of a certain scene; the mere likeness could be more perfectly achieved by the camera. It is rather a symbol of the artist's emotion on beholding a particular landscape, expressed in paint. And poetry, too, is symbolical: it is a collection of sensuous images which are really "words" in the secret language of the spirit.

July 9, 1909

The true æthete, according to Vernon Lee, the author of "Laurus Nobilis" (Lane. 3s. 6d. net.), should be an ascetic; and I am glad that this very able writer has done her best to correct the common impression that the æthete is necessarily a voluptuous person who is constantly crowning himself with roses, drenching his gullet with red wine, and generally behaving in the oddest possible manner. The fact is, of course, the asceticism of some kind—is necessary to any and every mortal achievement. I believe that Coventry Patmore says in one of his wonderful essays that you cannot have a good dinner without thinking: the thoughtless flesh, for instance; may cry out for a rich, thick soup; creaming, satisfying, delicious. But a higher power in the diner points out that that great bowl of "bisque" will take off the edge of appetite for the fish, dull the flavour of the entrée, make the vegetable a weariness, and the roast and salad a sheer impossibility. Consequently, the lobster soup is refused, and a few spoonfuls of a fine consommé take its place. And this is asceticism—of a sort; the rejection of the good for the sake of a better. So the athlete must be an ascetic if he means to win his race; he must deny himself all manner of pleasant things; and I have heard that jockeys are forced to undergo terrific penances on their path to perfection; perfection, in their case, consisting in light weight. And since the jockey, and the diner, and the Marathon runner are obliged to acquire a certain ascetic virtue, it may be easily imagined that a like rule applies to the higher world of the arts. There can be no perfect "æthesis" without some degree of "askesis": clear vision is not for bleared eyes.

July 16, 1909

"The glow of the Victorian era has faded"—so a recent critic tells us; but I hope that the recent critic is quite mistaken. Dickens, Thackery, Tennyson, Browning, Swinburne, Meredith have surely not become utterly obsolete and contemptible. There are lots of people who still read "Pickwick" and "Vanity Fair," and enjoy them, too. But I see that the critic quotes Tennyson as a prerogative example of his proposition. He says that Tennyson's philosophy was not profound, and that he had a prejudice in favour of domesticity. Well, it is not necessary that a poet should be a profound metaphysician, and there have been poets who have never once beaten their wives.

July 30, 1909

Here is an odd circumstance about the Shakespeare statuette recently "rediscovered," and, so far as I know, it has not been noticed. The point is this: Shakespeare leans against a little pile of books. Now, it is one of the "Baconian" commonplaces that the Stratford-on-Avon "rustic" was not clearly recognised in his own day as the author of the Plays. Mark Twain, latest—may I venture to hope the last—of the Baconians, puts the case in a nutshell: "I, Mark," he says in effect, "am well-known in Hannibal, Missouri, as the writer of certain works; and yet Shakespeare was so little thought of in Stratford-on-Avon that nobody knew much about him sixty years after he was dead—even in his own town." But the statuette with its pile of books is direct evidence that the "rustic" William Shakespeare was commonly reputed amongst his friends as the author of the Plays. Unless, by the way, those books are meant for the "Novum Organum," the Essays, and other works commonly attributed to Francis Bacon.

August 20, 1909

A recent article in T. P.'s WEEKLY dealt with the Holy Sepulchre—with relics in general—regarded as a matter of sentiment. There is a curious instance of this relic sentiment in the case of the Annual Dickens Exhibition now open at the Dudley Gallery in Piccadilly. Among the novelties of this years exhibition are such items as "The gun used by the novelist on the somewhat rare occasions when they went shooting," a presentation copy of "Master Humphrey's Clock," and an autographed letter on the subject of the Crimean War and spirit-rapping. There are other matters of the same kind; and, if one liked to talk "common sense," what a dreadful nonsense one could utter! "If you pretend to admire Dickens," one might say, "the best way to show your admiration is to read his books. There is more of the true spirit of Dickens in a page of 'Pickwick' than in a hundredweight of guns and presentation copies and letters about the Crimean War." This is quite true—and also gross impertinence. Like most impertinences and heresies it proceeds from a fundamental, deeply-rooted error as to the nature of things in general and of man in particular. If men were purely rational, they would not want to look at Dickens's fowling-piece or at Shakespeare's house at Stratford-on-Avon; but, since men are not purely rational, they are and will continue to be relic-worshippers.

September 3, 1909

The expected has happened. Mr. Chesterton's book on Mr. George Bernard Shaw has been reviewed by Mr. Shaw himself. And very pretty reading his article makes in that admirably edited journal "The Nation." The book, says Mr. Shaw, "is what everybody expected it to be: the best work of literary art I have yet provoked. It is a facilitating portrait study; and I am proud to have been the painter's model. It is in the great tradition of literary portraiture: it gives not only the figure, but the epoch. It makes the figure interesting and memorable by giving it the greatness and spaciousness of an epoch, and it makes it attractive by giving it the handsomest and friendliest personal qualities of the painter himself." That will please Mr. Chesterton. The review, as a whole, is less favourable. After dealing in very amusing fashion with what he calls Mr. Chesterton's anti-Puritan cry of "Beer for beer's sake," and with Mr. Chesterton's love of fairy tales (he says that his biographer has read only one fairy tale, "and that a mean one"—"Jack the Giant Killer"). Mr. Shaw proceeds:

> *Mr. Chesterton is, at present, a man of vehement reactions; and, like all reactionists, he usually empties the baby out with the bath. And when he sees me nursing the collection of babies I have saved from all the baths, he cannot believe that I have really emptied out their baths thoroughly. He concludes that I am a Calvinist because I perceive the value and truth of Calvin's conviction that once the man is born it is too late to save him or damn him: you may "educate" him and "form his character" until you are black in the face; he is predestinate, and his soul cannot be changed any more than a silk purse can be changed into a sow's ear. Next*

moment Mr. Chesterton is himself Calvinistically scorning me for advocating Herbert Spencer's notion of teaching by experience, and asks, with one of his great Thor-hammer strokes, whether a precipice can be taught by experience, to which I reply, in view of the new railway up the Jungfrau, that I should rather think it can. On another page he is protesting that I exaggerate the force of environment, because I proclaimed the staring fact that Christmas is a gluttonous, spendthrift orgie, foisted on us by unfortunate tradesmen who can just make both ends meet by the profits of the Christmas trade. He concludes that, in my joyless Puritan home (oh, my father! oh, my mother!), I never melted lead on "Holi-eve," never hid rings in pancakes, never did all those dreary, silly Christmas things, until human nature rebelled against them and they were swept out of our domestic existence, like the exchanging of birthday presents and the rest of inculcated tribal superstitions of the kitchen; and he would have me believe that every Christmas he turns his happy home into an imitation of the toy department at Gamage's, and burns a Yule log ordered, regardless of expense, from the Vauxhall ship-knackers. Chesterton, Chesterton, these are not the spontaneous delights of childhood: they are the laborious acquirements of bookish maturity. Christmas means: "Thank God Christ was born only once a year; so let us get drunk and have done with it for another twelve months." I would not give twopence for a Christian who does not commemorate Christ's birth every day and keep sober of it.

Mr. Shaw continues:

I must stop arbitrarily or my review will be longer than the book! For there is endless matter in G. K. C. My last word must be that, gifted as he is, he needs a sane Irishman to look after him. For this portrait essay beginning with the insanity of beer for beer's sake does not stop short of the final far madder lunacy of absurdity for absurdity's sake. I have tried to teach Mr. Chesterton that the will that moves us is dogmatic; that our brain is only the very imperfect instrument by which we devise practical means fulfilling that will; that logic is our attempt to understand it and to reconcile its apparent contradictions with some intelligible theory of its purposes; and that the man who gives to reason and logic the attributes and authority of the will—the Rationalist—is the most hopeless of fools; and all that I have got into his otherwise very wonderful brain, is whatever is reasonable and logical is false, and whatever is nonsensical is true.

September 10, 1909

Admirers of Miss Wilkins's beautiful New England stories will be pleased to hear the story of Basil Hayden, of Greenbrier, Nelson County. Nearly fifty years ago Basil swore that if Abraham Lincoln were elected President of the United States he would never step out of his room. Lincoln was elected, and Basil kept his word till his death a week or so ago. Basil was, undoubtedly, a harmless madman, but his story is strong confirmation of the New England character, as presented by Miss Wilkins. In one of her tales a man vowed that if a certain minister were chosen he would sit outside on the chapel steps every Sunday. He kept his vow for ten years and was rescued from it with great difficulty. The psychology of such characters is curious enough; it is, I suppose, Puritanism in extremis—the old fervour and resolution diverted from king-slaying and Quaker-hanging to ridiculous and trivial ends. The faith and resolution which once might have moved mountains now serve—to keep a man inside his house or outside his chapel.

September 24, 1909

The discovery of the body of the late Mr. John Davidson puts an end to a melancholy mystery. We now know exactly what he meant when he wrote his preface to his last volume, "Fleet Street and Other Poems," which has been issued by Mr. Grant Richards since his disappearance from his home on March 23 last. He went out in the evening to post the MS. of these poems to Mr. Richards, and was never seen again. The preface is as follows:

The time has come to make an end. There are several motives. I find my pension is not enough; I have therefore still to turn aside and attempt things for which people will pay. My health also counts. Asthma and other annoyances I have tolerated for years; but I cannot put up with cancer.

I thought that this might be my last book, and intended five poems, "Cain," "Judas," "Cæsar Borgia," "Calvin," and "Cromwell," under the general title, "When God Meant God," to be the principle contents. "Cain" is the only one of these poems which I have written. I should have concluded the volume with a second Testament in my own person, insisting that men should no longer degrade themselves under such appellations as Christians, Mohammedan, Agnostic, Monist, &c. Men are the Universe become conscious; the simplest man should consider himself too great to be called after any name.

John Davidson left a world for which his sympathies were already dead. He had written: "For half a century I have survived in a world entirely unfitted for me, and having known both the Heaven and the Hell thereof, and being without a revenue and an army and navy to compel nations, I begin definitely in my Testaments and Tragedies to destroy this unfit world and make it over again in my own image." This was the aim—of Davidson's last years. In an age of waning spiritual faith he sought to set up the beauty and perfection of Matter. He put forth this gospel in vain thunders, but with entire sincerity. Between the deafness of the world and his own troubles Davidson's fortitude—long tried and maintained—gave out.

October 22, 1909

Here is a curious instance of the difference in method between one writer and another. A few days ago Count Tolstoy paid a visit to Moscow, and of all those who called upon him he received only a self-taught peasant, who had been reading Tolstoy's novels.

To the peasant Tolstoy gave the good advice to write as slowly and as little as possible, and instanced his own case, saying that he rewrote everything at least seven times, and sometimes even more than seven.

But there is this difficulty about the giving of literary advice: that one man's meat maybe, as it were, the other man's poison. I have no doubt that his seven-fold process of "rectification" is the best of all methods for Count Tolstoy; but it by no means follows that it will prove to be the best method for the peasant.

December 3, 1909

The mass of criticism and cross-criticism already called forth by the event of Edgar Allan Poe's Centenary would perhaps have been spared were it generally realised that Poe, whose grandfather was a native Irishman, displayed, in life and work, simply the traits which make the Irish always the subject of misunderstanding. It is now the fashion to speak of the poet with a condescending indulgence which would pain his spirit more than any Griswoldian lie. But what faults he had were the usual concomitant of his virtues, only aggravated by the horrors he endured. He was passionate and Quixotic; proud, but easily touched by courtesy. He delighted in mystification. He had the Irish faculty of gathering knowledge from unsuspected sources, of building theories on the slightest premises; and he loved to astonish the world with a show of erudition, or to gain applause by a literary departure. It is interesting to trace through his stories, poems, and essays the influence of his Irish descent.

His characteristic mood is eminently Celtic. He was ever brooding on a faint and haunting dream of a past splendour, and he allowed his life to be directed by his dreams. He responded to the moods of Nature, but he saw the world chiefly in its autumn humour. He was oppressed by fear of some impending disaster, conscious of Fate, whose remote trafficking seemed ruthless to the individual, but he sometimes rose to a spiritual exultation that was almost prophetic. One might compare him with an Irish poet who explains the Druid wonder of Celtic poetry by the doctrine of the universal memory, just as Poe stated his philosophy in the strange, groping work "Eureka." Our Irish poet Mangan, again, is often compared with Poe, both with regard to his sad life-story and the technicalities of his verse. A favourite practice of Mangan was the repetition of the refrain, and Poe beautified his lyrics by the same device. It is likely the two poets were following, and one consciously, the other not, a common precedent. Poe was a wonderful master of sound; a foreigner might perceive the theme of "Annabel Lee" from the weird music of its meaningless words. And Gaelic poetry derives its charm and power from its peculiar verse—forms—its highly-developed rhythms, its assonance, and subtle play of words. Poe's work was fashioned on just the ideals of his ancestors in Ireland. Witness these lines:

A rosemary odour
   Commingled with pansies—
With rue and the beautiful
   Puritan pansies.

One fancies that had Poe lived to-day he would have been a leader in the Celtic revival. Perhaps, when the Irish character of his work is studied, some barren moralising on his personal character will be spared.

December 31, 1909

Speaking at the Christmas dinner of the Author's Club, Sir Oliver Lodge followed up a few rather sugary words concerning the genius of Mr. Anthony Hope with a characteristic plea. A work of literature, he suggested, was a really work of creation. The characters in a book ought not to be puppets, and it was unwise for a semi-cynical author to treat them at its close as if they were, and to talk of shutting them up again in their box. Certain great authors have been pleased to treat their characters in this manner, but Sir Oliver strongly disapproves. If they are properly created, he insists, these characters should have an independent existence of their own and a certain amount of free will and independence of action.

January 21, 1910

Some of my correspondents have been complaining of the difficulty of making a living out of literature. It may interest them, even if it does not console them, to learn that even that very popular Voltaire could not have paid his way if he had had to depend upon his pen. For most of his books he got no money at all, but only a few presentation copies; and the right of producing a complete edition of his collected works was sold during his lifetime for the ridiculous sum of £480. It was fortunate for him that he had a private income, derived from successful speculation in the army contracting industry, of about £14,000 a year.

Rousseau did rather better, but even he found that frivolous work and hack work paid better than literature and philosophy. His most successful composition was "Le Deven du Village," which may be fairly described as a musical comedy. The King gave him £216 for producing it before the Court at Fontainebleau. Madame de Pompadour gave him £108 for a performance at Bellevue. He got another £108 from the Opera, and £45 for the book rights: a grand total of £477. For his "Dictionary of Music" he asked £418 8s., but took part of the payment in the form of an annuity. His novels were not nearly as profitable. "La Nouvelle Héloïse" was the best novel that appeared in the pre-Revolutionary period. Everybody read it, and talked about it, just as, at a later date in England, everybody read and talked about "Waverley" and "Pickwick." But the author's share of the profits was only £198 8s.; and we encounter a further drop when we come to the case of "Le Contrat Social." This was the book which supplied the French Revolutionists with their doctrinaire philosophy. Rousseau got exactly £88 for it.

Truly times were bad for men of letters in those days. After the Revolution, though not immediately afterwards, they got better; and one may cite two notable successes—one of the history and the other of a romance. Thiers sold the copyright of his "History of the Consulate and the Empire" for £20,000; Victor Hugo got £1400 for each of the volumes of "Les Misérables," and the number of the volumes was ten. The publisher, it is true, lost on that transaction, but there is no record that that fact distressed the author.

April 8, 1910

I have been reading a report of a conversation between Mr. John Murray and a lady novelist on the subject of sex-problem novels. The lady said that the introduction of what were described as "these things" was necessary to "strong situations." Mr. Murray cited Scott's works as a proof that this was not the case. He might equally well have cited some of the novelists in those works "these things" figure to a considerable extent—he might even, for instance, have cited Zola. "These things" were an obsession with Zola, but he nevertheless did some of his strongest work when he got away from them. The scene at the end of "L'Assommoir," where Gervaise goes out onto the boulevards to beg and finds herself reaching out her hand for alms to the man whose faithful love she has rejected in happier days, is one of the most pathetic things in all literature—almost the only passage in Zola with the real "sense of tears" in it—and it owes nothing whatever to "these things."

April 15, 1910

A literary criticism that is likely to interest English readers is down to the credit of the Vicomte de Voguë, of the French Academy, who has just died, after a membership of twenty-two years. He is said to have proclaimed "Adam Bede" as superior, with all its faults, to any of the works of Flaubert or Stendahl, whose masterpieces, so he insisted, dealt only with the careful observation of externals. In George Eliot's work he professed to find "a beauty like the voice of God—that is all that I can say about it." He afterwards expanded this view in "Le Roman Russe," and the thesis which will he there unfolded came within an acre of bringing about the foundation of a new religion, "Neo-Christianity" being the name proposed for it by the Vicomte's enthusiastic disciples.

Appendices

After his departure from the *Evening News* in 1921, Arthur Machen ceased from regularly working on periodicals as a member of the writing staff. By this time, he was approaching his sixties when a new phenomenon occurred: the Machen boom of the twenties. During the first half of the decade, this upswell of interest, which had originated in America, gave Machen some overdue praise and income. Many of his books, some not issued since the 1880s, were reprinted for a growing audience. More importantly, this allowed long-completed, but previously unpublished works to see the printing press, including *The Secret Glory* (1922) and *Ornaments in Jade* (1924). This fame also encouraged new contributions to journals and magazines, some of which were former employers.

The first two items below were published in **T. P.'s and Cassell's Weekly**, a newer incarnation of the older periodical.

The last two pieces are of the earlier era, and both appear to be excerpts from articles Machen had written for the *Evening News*. The source articles have not yet been identified. It is quite possible that the namesake article of this collection, *Mist and Mystery*, is of similar origin.

What is the Artistic Temperament
(June 21, 1924)

There are all sorts of artistic temperaments. Some years ago a man of no artistic achievement committed a criminal action which involved the basest ingratitude to the best friend he had in the world. He was brought before the magistrate, whereupon a very eminent man of letters gave evidence in favour of this squalid criminal. "The scene," said he, "would appeal strongly to his dramatic sense."

Then there is artistic temperament as possessed by John Keats. He wrote "Odes About Grecian Urns and Nightingales" and bashed the offensive butcher of Hampstead.

If I Had One Wish
(December 4, 1926)

There is only one wise wish: the wish that we may like it when it comes; whatever "it" may be.

The Mysteries of Bread and Literature
T. P.'s Weekly (March 17, 1911)

When I read the statement of Dr. Frederick Gowland Hopkins the other day, I felt that the unlikely must surely come to pass. Significant phrases caught my eye, "certain at present unrecognised food substances," "substances of undetermined nature," "unknown substances," and so forth.

And it appears that, according to the highly eminent and expert authority of Dr. Hopkins, these mysterious and unknown substances may be the determining factor in the nutritive power of bread. . . . I think that everybody must feel that at last, when he has exhausted his logical or rational faculties on book or picture or cathedral, there is the mysterious remanet—the unknown quality which eludes all definition, which can scarcely be named intelligibly, which, for all that, is the one thing of consequence, the speck of leaven—returning to our loaves—which leaveneth the whole lump.

Take such writers as Dickens and Sir Walter Scott, by way of example. For the logical critic nothing is easier than to pull one or the other to pieces. It is simple to show that Sir Walter Scott had not the smallest understanding of the Middle Ages, that his style is slipshod, that his conduct of his tales is sometimes very slow, that his heroes are stilted and lifeless. So with Dickens; "a caricaturist," people say, and they point out that there are dialogues between Ralph and Nicholas Nickleby which are far more stilted and absurd than the most flamboyant speeches of the Crummles company.

Yet in each case there is that quality, unknown and mysterious, which makes Dickens and Scott supremely great masters. It is so with all literature, with all art, with all life; the real savours, the exquisite aromas are the effect of those "substances of undetermined nature," like in their effect to that Red Powder of the Alchemists, one grain of which would turn the heavy mass of useless lead to fine and glistening gold.

Appendices

The Cant of Cheerfulness
T. P.'s Weekly (April 7, 1911)

The demand addressed to serious and tragical writers to be always merry and bright moves me to ever increasing impatience. How would it have been with the history of the literature of the world if this advice had been given—and taken—in the past?

Imagine Isaiah advised thus: "Yes, you've got a certain knack of writing and some sense of style; but why not strike a more cheerful note: There's plenty of sunshine in the world; why not let us have it! Your work is so very depressing." . . . Let us clear our minds of this cant of cheerfulness. If a writer—such as Edgar Allan Poe—feels that it is his business to write of the tomb, then let him write of the tomb to the very best of his ability.

Order of Publication

T. P.'s WEEKLY

Vol. XII

"The Blue Saucer of Bristol." November 6, 1908, p. 599
  (Excerpted from The Literary Week)

Vol. XIII

A New Year Meditation. January 1, 1909, p. 17
Was Dickens a Socialist? January 5, 1909, p. 74
The Master Mystery. February 5, 1909, p. 180
The Occult World. March 19, 1909, p. 364
The Genius of Persia. March 26, 1909, p. 395
First Exchange: Machen & Ralph Shirley. March 26, 1909, p. 408
Many-Tower'd Camelot. April, 1909, p. 431-433
Second Exchange: Machen & Ralph Shirley. April 2, 1909, p. 448
A Study in Feminism. June 11, 1909, p. 754
The Church Pageant. June 18, 1909, p. 781

Vol. XIV

The English Renaissance. July, 1909, p. 42
The Holy Sepulchre. July 30, 1909, p. 141
G.K.C. on G.B.S. September 3, 1909, p.297
The Great Experiment. November 12, 1909 p. 627
The Life of the World to Come. November 12, 1909, p. 629
Trying the Spirits. December 3, 1909, p. 726

Vol. XV

Dee and Kelley. February 25, 1910, p. 233

Vol. XVI

Poe the Enchanter. October 28, 1910, p. 533

Vol. XVII

Mist and Mystery. February 24, 1911, p. 234

Vol. XXVI

Out of the Earth. November 27, 1915, p. 517-519

...

T. P.'s and Cassell's Weekly

Vol. I

Scrooge and the Spirit—of Psycho-Analysis. December 8, 1923, p. 228

Vol. VI

How to Enjoy Life. October 23, 1926, p. 827

ARTHUR MACHEN
Selected Works

FICTION

Novels

The Three Impostors (1895)

Hill of Dreams (1907)

The Terror (1917)

The Secret Glory (1922)

The Green Round (1933)

Novellas

The Great God Pan (1894) Includes *The Inmost Light.*

House of Souls (1906) Collection which includes *A Fragment of Life* and
The White People.

The Great Return (1915)

Short Story Collections

*The Angel of Mons: The Bowmen
and Other Legends of the War* (1915)

Ornaments in Jade (1924)

The Shining Pyramid (1925)

The Cosy Room (1936)

The Children of the Pool (1936)

Other Fiction

Eleusinia (1881) Poetry.

The Anatomy of Tobacco (1884)

The Chronicle of Clemendy (1888)

NONFICTION

Memoirs

Far Off Things (1922)

Things Near and Far (1923)

The London Adventure (1924)

Essays

Strange Roads (1923)

Dog and Duck (1924)

Dreads and Drolls (1926)

Notes and Queries (1926)

Tom O'Bedlam and His Song (1930)

Bridles and Spurs (1951)

Mist and Mystery (2022)

Miscellaneous Nonfiction

Hieroglyphics (1902) Literary criticism.

The House of the Hidden Light (1904) With A. E. Waite.

Dr. Stiggins, His Views and Principles (1906) Religious criticism.

War and the Christian Faith (1918) Christian apologetics.

Precious Balms (1926) Literary criticism.

The Canning Wonder (1925) Historical criticism.

A Reader of Curious Books (2020) Literary and antiquarian criticism.

Translations

The Heptameron (1886)

The Way to Attain (1889)

The Memoirs of Casanova (1894)

Casanova's Escape (1925)

Remarks Upon Hermodactylus (1933)

References

Bleiler, Richard J. *The Strange Case of "The Angels of Mons": Arthur Machen's World War I Story, the Insistent Believers, and His Refutations* (Jefferson, North Carolina; McFarland, 2015).

Dobson, Roger, Brangham, Godfrey, Gilbert, R. A. (eds). *Arthur Machen, Selected Letters* (Wellingborough, UK; The Aquarian Press, 1988).

Goldstone, Adrian & Sweester, Wesley D. *Bibliography of Arthur Machen* (University of Texas Press, 1965).

Machen, Arthur.
—*The Chronicle of Clemendy* (London; Martin Secker, 1926).
—*Notes and Queries* (London; Martin Secker, 1926).

Reynolds, Aiden & Charlton, William. *Arthur Machen* (London; The Richards Press, 1963).

Other Books by Arthur Machen

Available from Darkly Bright Press

The Great Return, Annotated Edition: Includes the classic novella, *The Sangraal, Parts I-III*, new essays and appreciations.

A Reader of Curious Books: A collection of rare material previously unavailable since its original 1887 publication in the *Walford's Antiquarian Magazine*.

Mist and Mystery: Recovered stories and essays by Arthur Machen from the pages of *T. P.'s Weekly*.

Available in 2023

Dreamt in Fire, The Expanded Second Edition: An original collection of Machen's fiction and essays which provides a comprehensive survey of his work.

Out of Print

A Secret Language: A miniature manifesto by Machen on his approach to literature and Christian mysticism. Annotated.

Levavi Oculos: The brilliant short story which highlights an application of Machen's literary theory. Annotated.

To place an order, please visit *darklybrightpress.com* and read rare Arthur Machen material posted every week.